DARK

MURDER

A gripping detective thriller full of suspense

HELEN H. DURRANT

JOFFE
BOOKS

Published 2016 by Joffe Books, London.

www.joffebooks.com

© Helen Durrant

ISBN- 978-1-911021-33-9

Prologue

Sixteen years ago

"Are you alright, son?" Just in the nick of time, the man pulled the small boy away from the edge of the footpath. "You mustn't stand so close to the road." He watched the lorry speed away. "That silly sod nearly had you."

Mavis Bailey's heart was beating fast as she pushed her husband's arm away from the boy's shoulder and knelt down beside him. "For God's sake, Paul, does he look alright?" she snapped at him. "He shouldn't be out here on his own for a start."

Good advice, but the boy didn't seem to understand. "Where's your mum, love? Have you lost her?" She looked up, catching her husband's eye. "Something's not right. Look at him: he's shaking, traumatised I'd say."

"He's wet too," Paul Bailey said, feeling the boy's clothes.

"That's because it's raining, you div."

"To get this wet he must have been wandering around for some time. Isn't he a bit young to be out alone?"

The boy was standing stock still on the footpath at the side of Link Road, the one that ran right through the middle of Oldston council estate.

"Pyjamas and wellies — it's an odd combination."

"Has something happened?" Mavis asked the boy gently. "Do you know where you live? Is your mum in one of these houses?" She looked round at the properties along the street. "Do you know which one it is?"

He didn't answer.

"He must have got out of the house on his own somehow," she said to her husband. "He must have been walking these streets for ages and got hopelessly lost. Give us your jacket, Paul, he's cold. We can't just leave him here." She looked up and down the deserted street. "Apart from the traffic, there's no one about."

"That's because it's only six thirty in the morning, woman. And why should there be? No one around here works. It's the place they dump the down and outs. These houses are full of the scum of Oldston."

Mavis ignored his comment for now. She took the coat and put it around the boy's shoulders. It was extra-large and swamped the small figure. "You'd think someone would be missing him by now," she said with concern. "The streets should be full of folk searching. What's your name, love?" Mavis turned him round so that she was looking at him full in the face. He was no more than about four. His eyes were wide open — staring straight ahead of him. He was crying silently, the tears making tracks down his grimy face.

"It's alright, we'll get you home," she reassured him, patting his back.

When he heard those words he screamed and shook his head. He would have run too but Mavis caught his arm and drew him close to her.

"He's scared stiff, shaking with fright. Ring someone," she told her husband, "the police perhaps."

"I've got to get to work. If I'm late again they'll dock my pay. Why don't you just knock on one or two doors? Someone's bound to recognise him."

Mavis shook her head. She had a bad feeling about the state the boy was in. He was dirty; he'd not seen water for a while. The pyjamas were too small for him, his thin arms and legs stuck out from the legs and sleeves. "Look," she said, pointing to his lower right arm. "Bruises. Looks like finger marks. Someone's been a little too heavy-handed."

"And not only there," Paul Bailey grimaced, looking closer at his neck.

Mavis opened the buttons on his pyjama top, "his chest and side are a mess. This kid's been beaten, and recently." Mavis felt sick. Who could do that to a small child? He was small, frail-looking and underweight for his age.

Paul Bailey lifted the pyjama top to look at his back. "Looks like cigarette burns," he practically whispered, "and there's dried blood on the top of his legs."

Mavis didn't want to believe what he was telling her. She shuddered, the images in her head turned her stomach. It was looking more and more like this child had been seriously abused. She nodded at her husband. "Get the police. They need to know about him. They'll tell social services and make him safe."

Chapter 1

Today

It wasn't the best way to start the week. A woman's body had been found on Oldston canal bank. It had been called in earlier that morning by a man on his way to work on the industrial estate nearby. Uniform had been first on the scene, then they'd called for CID.

DI Greco kept checking his watch as he waited for the pathologist to arrive. He wanted to get things moving and he couldn't do that until the pathologist said yes or no to murder. He stood alone outside the police tape. It was pouring with rain and bitterly cold. The body had been covered with a makeshift tent made from a trio of poles stuck into the ground and a tarpaulin.

Detective Inspector Stephen Greco had been with Oldston CID exactly three months. People were constantly asking him if he'd settled in yet. *Settled in*, what did they imagine the job was all about, for pity's sake? On the menu most days was a pick and mix of murder, rape, robbery and — already — one child abduction.

No, he was doing what he always did, coping.

So why do it at all? Why not find an easier way of earning a living? The answer to that one was easy: he wasn't capable of doing anything else; he was a policeman to the very core. The word *detective* ran through him like letters in a stick of rock, and he was good at what he did.

Oldston nick had recognised his talent from the off. He'd quickly earned himself a reputation as the new *hotshot* on the block. But recently the gloss had been wearing off. Not because of any work related issue — his clear up rate was excellent. The problem was, he didn't mix. He was still very much the mystery man. Greco gave nothing away; he didn't talk much about anything outside the current case and he never mentioned his family, a wife or anything. The nature of the job meant working long hours, and with a team. That was a hard ask for a man who was a natural loner.

His sergeant, Jed Quickenden, should have come to the scene with him, but yet again, when it mattered, he was late. If things didn't change then Greco would have to do something about that young man and it wouldn't be pleasant.

"Sir!" a raspy voice called out from behind him. "Sorry — couldn't help it. Bloody car wouldn't start and the bus was late." The young detective coughed his way to Greco's side.

Yet another feeble excuse. Greco wondered how long it had taken him to think that one up. Quickenden wasn't getting any better. He was a shirker of the first order, not something Greco appreciated or understood. He turned to look at him. The mouthed expletive as Quickenden stood in a patch of mud said it all. He looked dreadful. He was pale, untidy; his tie wasn't done up properly and his shirt hadn't been ironed. He looked as if he'd thrown on the first items of clothing he could find that morning. Even when Quickenden was on top form, he still looked odd. He was tall, well over six foot, and thin. His suit jackets were never quite long enough. His hair needed attention; he wore it too long for a policeman, and it was curly.

"Just as well you didn't drive, Sergeant. I can still smell last night's booze on you."

"Honestly, sir, it was only a couple in the Spinners." He sniffed at the arm of his jacket. "Must have spilt some."

The man was a joke. Jed Quickenden's reasons for joining the force were a mystery but one thing was for sure, they had nothing to do with fighting crime. He was young, lazy and more likely to dodge a case than get stuck in. Greco had been told that over the last five years Quickenden had worked with all three teams in the station but his workshy attitude meant he hadn't been encouraged to stay with any of them. Now they were trying him with the new boy.

The rest of his colleagues weren't people Greco would have chosen, either. They all had history. DC Grace Harper was a single parent with childcare issues. The information officer, Georgina Booth, seemed keen enough but she was a resource shared by all the other teams in the station. DC Craig Merrick was young and had been earmarked to rise through the ranks quickly. But all that early promise had evaporated when he'd come under suspicion of taking a bribe. Both Superintendent Wilkes and DCI Green had made no bones about it; part of Greco's remit was to mould them into shape. They wanted this ragtag bunch of no-hopers turned into a successful team. Problem was, he just wasn't a 'people person.'

"What do you see, Sergeant?"

"From here not much, sir, and we probably shouldn't even try. I never understood why we all race down to these incidents. We rarely get anything that helps. We should just wait for the experts to do their jobs and then weigh up what we've got."

"We're looking at the crime scene, Sergeant," Greco told him patiently, "so we look carefully, and we ask the basic questions. It is probable that that poor woman met her untimely end right here. Anything we see could turn out to be vital. For example, we're near enough to see she doesn't have a bag, and there are no other belongings lying around either."

"CSI will find everything there is. We're just two pairs of eyes."

Greco looked at him. "You've a lot to learn, Sergeant."

He watched Quickenden shrug that one off.

"We should ask what was she doing here — did she walk, was it part of her usual routine? If it was then did she live in one of the houses around here? Perhaps she had a dog with her and that's why she chose to walk along the canal bank. Then we have to ask if she didn't walk — how did she get here? There are no cars parked up except ours — so who brought her?" He looked at his sergeant, "perhaps you should make some notes — for later when we'll need the answers to those questions and more besides."

How he'd ever made sergeant in the first place was beyond Greco. He'd been given the nickname 'Speedy,' derived from the quick in Quickenden. Another joke, given the man's work record, and one that Greco didn't appreciate, nor did he like the use of nicknames much. He even objected when people called him Steve and not Stephen.

"Get on to Grace back at the station and ask her to check the missing person reports. We're interested in women reported in the last couple of days. If she has no belongings then identification is going to be the first problem." He looked at Quickenden. "What does that suggest to you, Sergeant?"

Quickenden shook his head — he'd no idea.

"A woman — no ID, no handbag or phone?" he asked quizzically. "I know what it suggests to me." His face went back to grim.

"Robbery," Quickenden decided.

"Could be, could well be a mugging gone horribly wrong."

"Or she could have been looking for drugs, sir."

"How so?"

"That bridge further up." He pointed. "That's where most of the dealing goes on around here."

"If it's that well known, then it's unlikely that your average middle-aged woman would choose to walk here alone."

Greco took his phone from his pocket, adjusted the settings on the camera function and took a couple of photos of the body. "Might help with identification," he enlightened Quickenden. "It'll be a few hours before the official pictures hit the system. In the meantime if we get a lead, these could be handy."

* * *

Jed Quickenden's day had started badly, and it wasn't set to get any better. The last thing he wanted was to partner the DI. He was well aware of his own shortcomings so there was bound to be trouble.

It would be a long hard slog and he'd get no peace.

It wasn't that Quickenden was deliberately lazy. The problem was his social life. What with the booze, and being unable to refuse that last game of cards in the pub, most nights he rarely got to bed before one or two in the morning. He kept telling himself he couldn't keep on living like this, but how to stop?

"Grace," he said, when the DC answered. "I'm stuck down by the canal with the boss." He walked a few yards away from Greco. "It's bloody wet and freezing cold, and he's obviously on a mission with this one. We've got a dead woman and we're waiting for the pathologist. He won't budge until one gets here, rain or no rain."

"Isn't that your job, Speedy?" she retorted. "Do us all a favour and pull your finger out — do some work for a change."

He pulled the phone from his ear holding it at arm's length as she ranted on. She could be a selfish cow. The number of times he'd covered her back when she'd been late. He made a mental note to revise that one. "Don't you bloody start; I've just about had enough." He shook his head; this was all he got these days — a load of backchat from the team and derisive remarks from them upstairs.

"It's fair comment, Speedy. You used to be better." Her voice was softer now, she was calming down. But she was right. There was a time when he'd been seen as the golden boy, the cop with the promising future. That was ages ago now, though. He'd actually got himself a bravery award back in the day, but since then his work record had gone steadily downhill.

He rubbed his head — it ached and Grace's ranting didn't help. That was the last time he'd drink any of Les's hooch, no matter how cheap or tempting. When he got back to the nick he'd need a gallon of coffee and a load of Paracetamol just to feel human again. "He wants to know about missing persons, women, in the last forty-eight hours. See what you can do, babe."

"Don't call me babe." She replied and rang off.

* * *

The more Greco saw of the ex-mill town, the more he disliked it. He'd come here after his marriage had collapsed, this was where his ex-wife Suzy had chosen to live. It wasn't that he harboured any romantic notions about winning the woman back; that boat had long since sailed. It was all about seeing their five-year-old daughter, Matilda, on a regular basis.

He'd moved to Oldston from Norfolk. The two environments were worlds apart. His patch in Norfolk had been rural, spread out. He'd loved the place and the warm, dry weather. The countryside had been a beautiful backdrop to his job, so different from the bleak grey that seemed to hang over Oldston.

In the cold and damp of an early spring morning he had to wonder what had motivated Suzy to move here of all places. It was so out of character. She'd been brought up on a farm near the Norfolk Broads and her parents still lived down there, retired now to the seaside at Cromer.

In complete contrast, Oldston was industrial — or it had been once. The remains of the cotton industry were visible everywhere; in the huge dilapidated, red brick mills scattered around the town and the rows of Victorian terraced houses that fanned out from the centre. Oldston's problem was that nothing had replaced the cotton industry. This meant there was nothing to mop up the vast pool of labour in the area. An underlying poverty pervaded the place, which Greco found depressing.

Suzy was renting a house in the Leesworth area — the more upmarket part of this godforsaken hole. Greco wasn't daft — there had to be a man at the bottom of it, but Suzy wasn't saying anything.

"Inspector!" A female voice called out from behind him, breaking into his reverie.

Greco and Quickenden turned to see a dark-haired woman in a white coverall coming towards them. She was carrying a doctor's bag and had a voice recorder in her hand.

"Doctor Natasha Barrington, home office pathologist from the Duggan Centre," she told them, taking some identification from her pocket.

"DI Greco and Sergeant Quickenden from Oldston CID," Greco said.

"Don't come any nearer without covering up," she instructed, handing out the suits and gloves. "I'll take a look; give you the basics and the have the preliminary report with you later today," she assured them, pulling up the hood on the suit.

"Suspicious death, or did she fall?" Quickenden asked hopefully, hauling his lanky frame into the coverall.

The pathologist ignored the comment and knelt down beside the dead woman. With her gloved hands she gently moved some of the dark hair that covered the side of her face. "The wound on her head is deep. I can see the skull," she noted into the voice recorder. "Also there are what looks like wood splinters embedded in the wound."

"There's your answer, Sergeant. Do you see anything made of wood here that she could have fallen onto?" Greco asked him.

"There are defence wounds on her hands," the pathologist continued. "This woman tried to fight someone off — perhaps her attacker," she told the pair. "I'd say she'd been dead since late last night — about eight hours. She looks about forty to forty-five years old."

The pathologist slowly rolled the body over a little further onto her side.

Greco, now suited up, moved forward.

"Is there anything to help with identification, anything lying under her?"

"There's no sign of any belongings under the body."

"Could you look in her coat pockets? Anything at all would help."

Natasha Barrington felt in both coat pockets and then put her hand into the inside one. "An ID badge. . ." She placed it in an evidence bag. ". . . In the name of Brenda Hirst. It appears she worked for Webb's Travel."

Greco noted down the name in his notebook.

"Also there are some nasty scratches on her wrist. I'd say a watch or bracelet had been ripped off her."

But it was the side of her face that had Greco's attention now. The cheek bones on the left side were caved in. It looked as if someone had stamped on her head.

"There is an imprint, Inspector," Natasha Barrington confirmed, "a boot with a thick, heavy tread."

He heard Quickenden cough and then retch. Natasha Barrington stiffened and said nothing for a few seconds. She'd moved the woman onto her back. Greco could hear her breathing as she knelt for a long moment, looking at the woman's face.

"I'll arrange for our CSI people to attend right away," she told them both soberly. "You should see this." She moved aside and beckoned Greco closer. "I think it removes any doubt about this being an accident," she said. "Her eyes are missing. From the look of the wound, I'd say they were gouged out deliberately."

Chapter 2

The woman's body went to the morgue at the Duggan Centre and Greco and Quickenden went back to the station. Neither man spoke much about what they'd seen. Both of them knew the score. Quickenden spent the journey mentally rearranging his week's social life. Basically clearing the decks because there was no way he'd get out of putting in the long hours the case would demand.

"Nasty," he said finally, as they pulled into the station car park. "Who does that sort of thing? What sort of monsters have we got out there?"

"The very worst, Sergeant, which is why we need to stay focused."

"Mind if I grab a bite in the canteen before I come up?"

"Take half an hour. We'll have a meeting at one o'clock, see what we've got."

Half an hour — the man's generosity knew no bounds! Mind you eating could be a problem; he still felt lousy from last night's session. He'd drunk far too much and on an empty stomach too, so now he was suffering for it.

One thing was for sure; he could do without the hassle of a new case, and partnering the DI would put him in the spotlight again — great! It would soon become glaringly obvious that his heart wasn't in it anymore. Quickenden's job set him apart from everyone he'd grown up with and he was getting tired of being the guy no one wanted to talk to. A lot of his schoolmates had turned to crime after long spells of unemployment and Quickenden knew the score — he was a cop so they no longer trusted him. It was a situation that he was uncomfortable with particularly as he still liked to socialise with most of them.

As usual, the canteen was busy. He scanned the tables for someone he could foist himself on and spotted DC Grace Harper in the queue for food.

"Grace!" he called to out to the pretty blonde. "There'll be no peace now, it's a real bad 'un." He grimaced, standing beside her. "Eyes missing, nearly threw up — never seen owt like it."

"D'you mind Speedy, I'm about to eat." She pulled a face.

"He'll really be on one now. He'll have us here at all hours. Greco'll have us running around like scalded cats, and then he'll just go and double check everything himself. The man's an obsessive."

"He's bloody good and like I said earlier, you need to straighten yourself out. Try to be a bit more like him."

"Please no!" He feigned shock. "Why on earth would I want to do that?"

"Because you're going nowhere, being like you are now. Don't you want promotion — a leg up to DI, your own team?"

"No way — I'd have to move."

"And look at the state of you, Speedy, you're a disgrace. He won't have it, not for much longer. Mess up on the case as well as continuing to look like a washing basket gone wrong and you'll be out."

Speedy knew she was right, but did he really care? The job was a real pain in the arse at times, and he was on a bit of a roll at the Spinners, his local pub. He and some mates had a card game going. Over the last few nights he'd cleared over a ton, with precious little effort. He could see why some of his mates were workshy — they didn't have to bother.

"Pie looks nice — they make it here," Grace told him.

"Don't know if I can — my guts are bad. Anyway if it's so nice why aren't you having it?" He was looking at her plate of salad.

"Some food might settle you. It's going to be a long day," she warned, ignoring his observation.

"Okay — get me some, will you, and I'll get us a table," he offered.

"Come on, Speedy, out with the money." She held out her hand, flexing her fingers. "I'm not some sort of soft touch who'll fall for your little boy lost routine."

No, she wasn't and that was a pity because he liked Grace. Trouble was she had more sense than to like him back.

* * *

There were times when Speedy got on Grace's nerves. He could have had it all yet all he ever did was squander his chances. He'd made sergeant in no time flat, whereas for her it was going to be a long hard slog.

Grace was ambitious. Before she'd had Holly she'd had a plan that would see her at the top of her game by the time she reached forty. But that was out of the window now. There was no way she could do that and raise Holly on her own. Her mother helped, she was a marvel, but she had her own life to lead.

Every morning, Grace felt guilty when she dumped Holly with either the breakfast club at school or with her mother. She wanted to be a good detective, and she knew she had it in her to be one of the best. But all her DI saw was a DC who was usually late and the first to leave given half the chance. Speedy didn't know he was born, yet all he did was abuse his opportunity.

"Like I said, you're not eating much." He grinned at her as he shovelled the pie down his throat.

"This will do me for now," Grace sighed, sitting down. "For someone who wasn't hungry, you've made short work of that."

"Like you say, it'll be a long day."

Grace pushed the lettuce leaves and tomato around her plate. Speedy was right, she didn't eat very much. Her mother said she was too thin and needed some meat on her bones. But Grace liked the way she looked. She was slim, she had a straight up-and-down figure that was almost boyish. On the days she wore jeans and a shirt, from behind it was only her long blonde hair that gave the game away. People said she was pretty, but Grace was a realist. The trials and tribulations of life had hardened her features. She looked like the sort of woman who'd stand no nonsense. Pity she hadn't always looked that way. In her younger days, she'd had to put up with enough 'nonsense' to last her a lifetime.

* * *

Georgina Booth was the information officer for CID at the station. She wasn't attached to a particular team but worked where she was most needed. However if Georgina was given the choice she would have chosen to stay with DI Greco on a permanent basis. She liked his style, he got things done and this suited her no nonsense approach.

She took her work seriously, throwing herself into whatever case was current. Georgina didn't attract the attention that Grace did. She wasn't attractive for a start. She was small and dumpy with dark hair which she wore cut short. Grace could have a laugh with the others, and they liked her. Georgina didn't have that sort of confidence. She was far more serious and, given the job, didn't think there was a lot to laugh about. She didn't wear a uniform but always dressed in a skirt and white blouse. Georgina, or George, liked her job, the only trouble was — she was spread a little thin.

She'd tried her hand at regular police work; she'd made CID and been a DC like Grace a couple of years ago but she couldn't hack it. Being out there, on the job, seeing life in the raw had taken its toll. George had made the decision to stick to a desk job — it was safer.

While Greco and Quickenden were out, she and Grace had looked at the latest list of missing persons. Two of the names fitted the description of the dead woman.

* * *

Brenda Hirst and Rose Donnelly were both fortyish. Brenda had been reported missing by her husband, Jack, and Rose by a friend who hadn't wanted to leave a name. Greco took the mobile from his pocket and flicked through the dozens of snaps. The last two were of the woman.

The victim wore a beige three-quarter length raincoat, and a black pleated skirt. He couldn't see her top. Her shoes were black, heels low and chunky. She wasn't dressed for a night out on the tiles — so where had she been? More importantly, what had happened to take her along the canal bank, which was well known, according to Quickenden, for being a dangerous place?

"Do we know anything about either of these women?" he asked Grace when she returned from lunch.

"Rose Donnelly was done for shoplifting about two years ago," she told him.

"Dig out the file and leave it handy. There may be nothing in it but these women are roughly the same age and went missing at the same time."

Greco sent the photo he'd taken of the victim to the printer and stuck the image in the dead centre of the incident board, fiddling around until he got it exactly right.

As the seconds passed, Suzy's voice echoed in his head. Let it go Stephen or it'll rule your life. He gave the image one last tweak and walked away. She was right; his OCD was taking over again. Stress, he reckoned but what could he do about that? It came with the job.

He walked out, he needed to take five minutes, get his head together before the briefing. Greco made for the gents toilet. He leant forward over one of the sinks and took several deep breaths. Suzy's words were still ringing his head. But it wasn't that easy. She had no idea what he went through. He turned on the tap holding his hands under the steady stream of hot water. He held them there for several minutes, every few seconds using the liquid soap from the dispenser to scrub off imaginary dirt. This was stupid, so why couldn't he stop?

"Okay, sir?" DC Craig Merrick asked. He'd come in to wash his hands, and Greco hadn't even noticed until he'd spoken.

Greco nodded, but as he caught his own reflection in the mirror he could understand why the man had asked — he was white. The colour had literally drained form his face. "Just cleaning up — it was a hard one this morning."

Walking back to the office, Greco felt his heart pounding. If he couldn't get it under control he'd have to see someone about it — again.

Once back he looked around; Grace, Georgina and Craig were all back from lunch and busy working, but there was no sign of Quickenden. Greco looked up at the office clock — he'd taken almost an hour now. He wrote the name 'Brenda Hirst' neatly next to the photo on the board followed by a question mark.

"Sorry, sir," Quickenden apologised, as he barged through the office door. Greco could see that he was out of breath. He'd obviously run up the stairs.

Greco said nothing — he'd deal with him later.

"Grace, do you have the Hirsts' address?"

"They live quite near where she was found, sir," she noted, handing him the sheet.

"Could have been a domestic." Quickenden threw this into the pot. "Irate husband does in the wife then goes berserk — well, with whatever he took her eyes out with."

Greco did not appreciate the humour. "We'll go and talk to him," he said, looking directly at his sergeant. "And while we're there keep the facile comments to yourself, understand?"

"It's not facile, sir, it could well be a simple case of a domestic," Quickenden reiterated. "A row, a fight, and she ends up on the canal bank."

"It says on the report that when Jack Hirst reported her missing he was asked if his wife might simply have left him. But he was adamant that she wouldn't do that. He reckoned they were solid," Grace told him, reading from the sheet.

Greco rolled his eyes. "She was killed several hours after she'd left work. She went somewhere, and not with her husband. And don't you believe all you hear about marriage, Constable. They all have their problems."

Quickenden had not been listening. He was rattling around in one of his desk drawers looking for something. Greco saw him wink at Grace Harper.

"Get a move on, Sergeant," Greco barked.

"Just tidy myself up a bit, sir," he replied.

"Tidy hair won't fix things," he warned.

Greco saw the looks exchanged between Grace and Quickenden. She was doing her best to warn him to tone it down — it showed in her body language.

"Sorry if this wasn't what you have in mind for today. I don't imagine that partnering the DI is something you enjoy but it's in the job spec, Quickenden," Greco put to him sarcastically. "We have a job to do and I am going to be on your back day and night until we've cracked this. So sort yourself out."

"I'll go to barber's later — get it cut," he said with one last look in the mirror.

"I'm only interested in the case, Sergeant, not your hair."

"A bloke has an image to keep up, sir. There was a bird in the Spinners the other night who really liked it. She sat on my knee and ran her fingers through my mane."

Greco shook his head. He didn't have an office of his own so he'd chosen a desk as far away from the others as he could get. But the inane chatter he was constantly privy to drove him up the wall, and was a first class waste of time.

"Grace, get hold of the CCTV footage from around Webb's Travel where Brenda Hirst worked on the High street and have a look at it," he barked sharply. "You should have sobered up by now, sergeant, so you can drive. You know the town far better than I do." Greco threw him a set of car keys.

* * *

"Did you hear that comment?" Grace asked Georgina once the two had left the office. Our leader seems to have a jaundiced view of marriage."

"He's recently divorced, that's why," Georgina Booth told her. "Something I overheard when he was chatting to the DCI." She shrugged. "But that's all I know; he doesn't give anything away."

Grace was well aware of that. Stephen Greco kept things to himself — not something she appreciated. Grace liked to know exactly what was going on in her colleagues' lives, and that included their new DI.

All she knew was what she saw. He was young, well, youngish; certainly no more than forty; and — the icing on the cake — he was something of a dish. He was tall, well built, with the sort of physique that suggested he worked out. He had blue eyes and blond hair that fell in a boyish fringe that half covered his forehead. He was always immaculately dressed: suit, crisp white shirt, and tie. If he was free and single, then Grace wanted to know.

Her mother was always going on at her to get herself a man, someone permanent who would be a father to Holly. Grace wasn't sure. She liked men, but did she want one in her life all the time? She had managed perfectly well on her own for the last six years. Not that it was easy, because it wasn't. It was wing-and-prayer stuff most of the time, where work was concerned. Something else her mother was critical about. Grace knew she'd like nothing better than for Grace to give up, take time out to raise Holly *properly*, as she put it. But in Grace's opinion that was a load of rubbish. Grace needed the money, but she also loved the job and given half a chance, she'd be good at it.

"Do you reckon he's seeing someone? Is that why his marriage failed?"

"God no! His marriage failed, idiot, because of how he is. He's a complete dork. All that tidiness and obsessing about the cleanliness of the place." Georgina shook her head. "He was here this morning well before it was light. When I arrived, he was checking the waste bins had been emptied and cleaned. He gave Dora the one from the kitchen and asked her to bleach it."

The two women started to laugh. He was different, that was for sure.

"Perhaps the love of a good woman could change him — make him loosen up a little."

"It'll take more than that — he'll have been like that forever, believe me."

"Still, if he asks . . ." Grace smiled.

"You've got enough on your hands as it is. The job, your little girl; you're a single parent, isn't that tough enough without taking on him as well?"

Georgina was right. It was all Grace could do to keep up as it was. It was only a matter of time before Greco would be hauling her over the coals too because of her timekeeping. If Holly was ill, or Grace's mother cried off then Grace often didn't come in until after lunchtime, if at all. The previous DI had turned a blind eye — he'd understood, up to a point. But Grace couldn't see Greco being as lenient.

* * *

The Hirsts lived just on the outskirts of Oldston centre. The houses were little two-up two-down cottages crammed together with no front gardens. In contrast to the rundown area the Hirsts' house looked neat and tidy. There was newly fitted double glazing, and the brickwork had recently been re-pointed.

A middle-aged man answered the door.

"Mr Hirst?" Greco asked, flashing his badge. "DI Greco and DS Quickenden from Oldston Police. May we come in?"

The man looked upset. His face was drawn and his eyes bloodshot from lack of sleep. "Have you heard anything? She's been gone nearly all weekend. Have you found her?" Jack Hirst asked the pair hopefully.

Greco shook his head — sadly that wasn't the case. "Sergeant, go make us a cup of tea," he suggested, nodding towards the kitchen.

Hirst led the way into the small sitting room and gestured for Greco to sit down.

"She's never done anything like this before. I don't understand," he said running a hand through his greying hair. "She doesn't go anywhere much, apart from the knitting circle and work." He shook his head. Greco could see that this had him stumped.

"We'd talked about having a holiday this year. Brenda had said the Channel Islands, but I wasn't sure. When she was late back on Saturday I thought perhaps she'd gone to get some brochures. She'd said she'd call in at the travel agents after work."

Hirst looked unkempt. His clothes were crumpled and marked as if he'd worn them night and day all weekend. He hadn't shaved either.

"I rang them, the travel agents, but they haven't seen her. She left work at the usual time so why didn't she come home? Why no word? This isn't like Brenda at all."

Now for the hard part. "Mr Hirst, Jack, earlier today we found the body of a woman on the canal bank . . ." There was no prettier way to wrap up news like this. It was better to tell it straight.

Silence.

The man stared at Greco as if he hadn't understood the words, and then he seemed to fold, to crumple, his entire body shrinking into the sofa as he wept softly. Greco watched. It was obvious that Jack Hirst couldn't get his head around this at all.

"Accident?" he asked finally, sobbing into a hankie.

"I'm afraid not, Jack," Greco replied gently. "The woman we found had been murdered."

Jack Hirst covered his face with his hands, howling with a mixture of what sounded like disbelief along with the grief. "Then it won't be Brenda," he cried emphatically. "It can't be, there's been some mistake. Who'd want to murder Brenda? It doesn't make any sense."

"We found her ID badge from work in her coat pocket. It had her photo on it and her name."

"I still say there's been some mistake. I want to see her. If I see her then I'll know. But it won't be her; no one would do that to my Brenda."

"Jack, I'm going to have to ask you a few questions. We want to catch whoever did this as quickly as we can."

Hirst stared at him blankly. Had he even heard?

"When she left home, was everything okay?" Greco asked, taking his notebook from his coat pocket. "No problems that you are aware of? She wasn't upset about anything?"

"No, of course not, everything was fine, we were fine," he assured him. "We're always fine. There was nothing going on, everything was, well, just ordinary," he added.

"I presume your wife has a mobile phone?" Quickenden asked, entering the room with the tea.

"Yes, and she had it with her. I've been ringing it constantly but it goes straight to messaging."

Quickenden put the tray of tea on a small table and handed the cups around.

"Did she use a computer, laptop or tablet?"

Greco noted that his sergeant was asking the right questions. If he could smarten up his appearance and get up in the mornings, then perhaps there was a career for him yet.

Hirst shook his head. "We don't have anything like that. She has enough technology to deal with at work. When she gets home, Brenda likes to relax. She likes her telly programmes and she knits, well, knitted." He picked up her knitting bag from the side of the chair and clutched it to his chest. "She won't be knitting any more now, will she?" He began to sob again.

"Do you have a recent photograph of Brenda, Jack?"

The room fell silent as Jack Hirst put his teacup on the table and took a silver photo frame from the sideboard and handed it to Greco.

The DI looked carefully at the image in front of him, seeking out resemblances between it and the body they'd seen earlier. It was difficult. This photo showed a pleasant-looking woman with dark brown hair, a wide smile and a plump face. The body had taken a beating — the bones of the face had been broken and the eyes were missing. However, the photo did match the ID they'd found.

"What was Brenda wearing that morning when you saw her last?"

"It was wet; she had on her raincoat, the shortish one with the belt around the waist."

"Colour?"

"Beige," he replied. "She had on the skirt she'd bought at the market the week before, the black one."

In normal circumstances, Greco would have asked him to identify the body but he couldn't put this man through an ordeal like that. He'd see if there was anything the pathologist could do. The last thing he wanted was to upset this man any more than he had already.

"Is there anyone who can stay with you, Jack?" Quickenden asked.

"We have no children and no siblings either, it's always been just me and Brenda against the world." He attempted a wan smile.

"I can arrange something, a PC to stay. They would keep you up to date with our progress."

"Yes, okay, but not a woman. If I have to have someone, then make it a bloke."

"Rest assured that we will do everything in our power to catch whoever did this."

"I still think it's a mistake."

"There will be more questions but we'll try not to upset you more than necessary."

"If this is right . . ." He paused for a moment. "If my Brenda has been murdered then you can ask anything — you don't have to spare my feelings. I want the bastard catching. Do you understand?"

Greco nodded. "The ID was from Webb's. Is that where Brenda worked?"

"Yes, she's — was — a receptionist there. They're on the High Street; the coach holiday company. She's been with them over ten years. It's hard work and she gets frustrated with it at times but mostly it suits — suited her."

"How did she get there and back, did Brenda drive?" Quickenden asked.

"No, she always walked. It's not far really, just down the road then onto the High Street."

"Did Brenda contact you at all on Saturday — any missed calls for example?"

He shook his head. "She doesn't ring me from work; it would be odd if she did."

"Where do you work, Mr Hirst?"

"I used to work at Frasier's. You know the engineering works on the industrial estate by the canal. Before they went bust."

"So, you're currently unemployed?"

He looked at Greco and coughed. "No — breathing problems; COPD," he explained. "Chronic obstructive pulmonary disease, got from years of working in a fume-filled workshop, and smoking, of course." He coughed again.

"Do you have any financial problems because of that?"

"No, none — we're okay for money. We live simply and we've always saved. We just get on with things."

"Can I take this?" Greco asked, holding up the photo.

Jack Hirst nodded.

"Do you know a woman called Rose Donnelly?" Greco asked, removing the photo from the frame. "Could she have been a friend of Brenda's?"

"I don't know the name. Should I?"

Greco shook his head. "No matter, it was just a thought."

* * *

"D'you believe him, sir?" Quickenden asked when they were outside.

"I don't disbelieve him, Sergeant, but I prefer to gather evidence and analyse it before I make up my mind about anything."

Quickenden groaned inwardly. Now it was starting. Greco had a reputation for being methodical, but it was more than that, he was finicky. He checked every little detail — sometimes twice.

"He's really cut up about what's happened. He wasn't putting that on, sir."

"Of course he wasn't, Sergeant. His wife was murdered. How would you react?"

"Point taken."

"But we can't let him see her, not like that. The image would stay with him forever."

So he had a heart. He'd been okay with Jack Hirst too. He'd used his first name at least once, Quickenden had observed. Perhaps the boss was a closet softy after all.

"Nonetheless we must keep an open mind until the evidence tells us different, Sergeant. He could be emotional for any number of reasons."

"True. It could be a domestic, but I doubt it somehow."

"Your instinct twitching, Sergeant?"

Quickenden didn't know how to answer that, but the DI was right. He didn't think Hirst had anything to do with the death of his wife and it had nothing to do with proof.

"Is it back to the nick, then?"

"No. I think we'll go and speak to Brenda Hirst's employers — see what they have to throw into the pot."

"Sir . . ." the DS began and cleared his throat nervously. "Sorry about this morning. I know I wasn't up to the mark. After the weekend I've had, I didn't have my mind in gear."

"That happens a lot, doesn't it?" Greco observed dryly. "You were going in the right direction back there. You asked a few well-chosen questions. But you are a long way from being a reformed character. Look at the state of you. Your shirt looks as if you spilt your breakfast down it and you're bleary eyed from last night's drinking session. Bet you didn't get to bed before the early hours, did you?"

Quickenden sighed and turned away. If your face didn't fit, the inspector was a bastard. "Sorry, sir. It won't happen again." It was unconvincing.

"That's just the trouble, son; it will, and we both know it," came the blunt reply.

Chapter 3

"This will be about Brenda's disappearance." Caroline Dulwich greeted both detectives with this announcement as she led them into her office.

While they had been waiting, they'd been treated to the rumours circulating about the new office manager. Greco was told that Caroline Dulwich had embraced the post at Webb's Travel with more enthusiasm than her colleagues were comfortable with. She was bossy, a woman full of her own importance. She'd taken over the role from an individual she'd considered to be inept and totally wrong for the job. Apparently, Brenda had felt intimidated by her.

The current receptionist at Webb's Travel had been only too happy to give the pair chapter and verse. Greco didn't like gossip as a rule, but in this case it did give an insight into the work side of Brenda Hirst's life.

Now they understood the staff's complaints. Her attitude grated. Once the office door was firmly shut behind them, she sat down behind an imposing desk and with an imperious wave of her hand, gestured for them to sit on the other side.

"She's wasting everyone's time, you know," Mrs Dulwich continued. "She'll have gone off with that chap of hers, and who can blame her. Life with that bore she was married to was turning her into a frustrated old bat. Believe me he was driving her into an early grave."

Greco felt he should stop her now, but this was quite a revelation. Jack Hirst had painted such a different picture. The woman he'd described was a stay at home wife who loved her husband and was happy with her lot. One of them had got it very wrong, but which?

"You know for sure that there's another man?" Greco asked, fishing his notebook out of his pocket. "Only Mr Hirst isn't aware of anything untoward in their marriage."

"Well, he wouldn't, would he?" Brenda replied scornfully. "She isn't stupid. Brenda's careful, secretive," she confirmed, with a nod of her head. "But there's definitely someone. There's the phone calls, regular as clockwork and she always goes out into the yard at the back to take them."

"So this person, whoever it was, rang her on her mobile?"

"Mostly, but he rang the main office phone too, once or twice, that's how we know," she explained. "I believe one of the girls did try to speak to Brenda about it but she wouldn't divulge anything. Very suspicious if you ask me — that's when the rumours started."

"Did she know that her colleagues were talking about her?" the sergeant asked.

Caroline Dulwich pulled a face, "She must have done, and there was enough teasing. You see, Inspector, we were all surprised. Brenda isn't the type. She's not glamorous; she doesn't wear fancy clothes or much make-up. Frankly, I was gobsmacked when I found out that she, of all people, had got herself another man."

"Do you know who he is, would any of her colleagues know?"

She shook her head. "I doubt it, Inspector. Tight-lipped, that's Brenda." She shook her head. "You're wasting good money and resources looking for her. They'll have gone off somewhere warm together, mark my words, the woman has done a runner."

"I'm afraid not." Greco sighed, wishing it was true. "You see, Mrs Dulwich, Brenda Hirst was found dead this morning. We are looking for her killer, not investigating a missing person."

She went pale. The news sank in and she fished in her desk drawer for a tissue. "That's dreadful," she whispered. "The others will be devastated. I know I can waffle on, but we're a tight-knit crew really."

"Was Mrs Hirst popular?" Greco asked. "Did she get on with the other staff and the customers?"

"Yes, after a fashion. I mean we all tried to like Brenda," she replied guardedly. "I know it's going to sound churlish given what's happened but Brenda wasn't easy to like. I don't enjoy saying it but it's a fact. She was hard on the coach drivers when it really wasn't necessary. But then it's no picnic, you know, standing out there day after day dealing with the folk around here. They're rude, and they swear a lot. If you can't sort their problems at the speed of light they complain," she told them.

"You're busy then, your holidays are popular?"

"Yes and for very good reasons. We give value for money. We offer people travel in the UK and Europe. We run a fleet of luxury coaches and accommodation at decent hotels, and all for a fair price. But what makes us different is that we offer our customers a payment plan and that's popular. But things are tough. People pay the deposit, a couple of payments, then renege on the balance. Mr Percival says if there's no insurance, we should sue, but we'd be suing half the town if we did that."

There was resentment in her tone. Was it because of a particular incident, Greco wondered?

"Had Brenda upset someone recently?" he asked.

"Not enough to kill her, if that's what you mean." Caroline Dulwich shrugged. "But she was a cold fish. She couldn't help it. It was just her way. We see a lot of upsetting stuff, poverty you know. People see our adverts, the offers we have and they forget it all has to be paid for. But Brenda had no sympathy. They want to book a holiday, so that's what she does and she'd pile on the extras too. You know — sea views, extra excursions, stuff a lot of folk round here definitely can't afford."

"Who is Mr Percival?" Greco asked her.

"Percival Webb, the owner. He and his son, Nathan, run the business. Well, Nathan is learning the ropes at present, he's a little young to shoulder any big responsibilities. The business was started forty years ago by Mr Percival and his father. Once Nathan knows the score then Mr Percival will retire, I expect."

"Was there an incident recently?" Quickenden asked, nodding at the office next door.

"The Roberts family, that wasn't good," Caroline Dulwich shook her head. "It had been a hard day, we were rushed off our feet and then in they came," she pulled a face. "We have irate mothers and screaming kids all the time, but this was different, and Brenda should have seen that. The whole thing should have been handled differently."

"What happened?"

"Well, nothing, and that was the problem — Brenda sent Mrs Roberts away with a flea in her ear. The woman swore blind she'd been in and booked a holiday for the lot of them to Torquay and paid a deposit. But there was nothing on the system. There were no more places either, the coach was full. With hindsight, it would have been better if Brenda had tried to compromise, offered them an alternative, but she didn't. Brenda decided they'd need to write in and provide proof of the original booking before anything could be done." Caroline Dulwich shrugged. "Brenda could be her own worst enemy at times. She had to get into an argument with the angry woman, didn't she?" She sighed wearily.

"Was Brenda always confrontational?"

This didn't match the ordinary, rather staid woman that Jack Dobson had described earlier.

"More often than not," she replied soberly. "To be fair the Roberts are a difficult family. It comes with the poverty, the deprivation. They'd saved up and parted with good hard cash for the deposit and there was Brenda virtually telling them to get lost."

"Thank you, Mrs Dulwich, you've been very helpful." Greco smiled. "We'll arrange for the other staff to be interviewed over the next couple of days," he added. "If you could arrange a space, a small room somewhere, it'll just take a few minutes of everyone's time, nothing heavy," he assured her.

"Revenge," Quickenden suggested once they were outside, "the Roberts woman getting her own back and going too far?"

"That's sounds a bit far-fetched, Sergeant. It was only a holiday booking, after all."

"But you heard that woman, folk around here are quick to react, they get fired up."

"No, the phone calls are a much better bet. If Brenda Hirst did have another man, we need to find him."

"Or the man who rang her could have been a tradesman, but Caroline Dulwich and others have jumped to conclusions and think she has a lover," Quickenden suggested. "But if Caroline Dulwich is right, then I'm surprised her husband has no idea, sir."

"We don't know that. We only know what he's told us," Greco pointed out.

"In any case, we need to speak to Jack Hirst again. He said she hardly went out. If she had another bloke on the go, when did she see him?"

"Good to see you getting your brain into gear, Sergeant," Greco noted. "She went to knitting club. We will speak to Hirst again and we'll check out the club too. She could have been using it as a cover. But we need to interview her colleagues and do some digging to make sure. If she was having an affair, then someone will know."

"So, if she did have a fancy man, is he in the frame d'you reckon, sir?"

"At this point we've no way of knowing. I don't think it's wise to make any assumptions," Greco said. "All we can say for sure is that she's dead — murdered. Also that something happened to her between leaving the office at five on Saturday and her husband reporting her missing at seven thirty."

"It's not long, sir, is it? A couple of hours late, that's all."

"It's long enough."

"Her husband said she always went straight home. She's a creature of habit, day after day everything follows the same routine."

"Except for Saturday. Whatever happened to Brenda Hirst on Saturday was not routine."

They walked long the High Street until they reached the travel agent that Brenda had visited on Saturday. Greco and Quickenden flashed their warrant cards. "We're interested in this woman," Greco told the assistant, showing her Brenda Hirst's photo. "She may have been in here sometime on Saturday."

"I know Brenda," the young woman replied. "Her husband was in asking about her, but no, we didn't see her, sorry."

"Did you see her pass by, on her way home perhaps?" Quickenden asked.

"I can't say. To be honest I don't remember. There is CCTV along the street, you could look at that," she suggested.

"Don't worry, we've got someone on it."

"Back to the nick, sir?" Quickenden said when they left.

Greco nodded.

* * *

DC Grace Harper had been looking at the CCTV from the High Street. She and Craig Merrick, another DC with the team, had been poring over it for what seemed hours. They saw Brenda Hirst leave work at lunchtime. Not terribly informative; all she did was pop along to a supermarket further up the street from Webb's and return with two carrier bags. At five, the cameras caught her at the main entrance where she appeared to be waiting for someone.

"Sir!" Grace called, "this looks interesting."

"She's waiting — see there, now she's waving. She's looking across the street — a lift perhaps?"

"She walks home as a rule," Quickenden reminded them.

"She does have two heavy-looking shopping bags. Speedy, someone might have offered her a ride home," Grace suggested.

Greco had to admit it did look as if she was getting a lift. But with who? "First thing tomorrow we'll speak to the staff at Webb's. Grace, ring the office manager, Caroline Dulwich; make sure she's set it up. She thinks Brenda had a man — check if anyone can add to that. Also check who was in there Saturday afternoon. For now go and talk to the shopworkers in that area, see what they remember. Get your hands on any other CCTV available and we'll go from there."

Greco went across to the incident board. He made several notes beside Brenda's photo and then added the name, 'Rose Donnelly.'

"She has been reported missing. The informant was a woman but she wouldn't give a name," Grace told him. "She has money, sir. Rose Donnelly recently inherited a small fortune. She lives alone, no husband, never married and no boyfriend as far as we can tell."

"Does she work?"

"Not as far as we know, sir."

"But you have her address?"

"Yes, she lives on the Link estate."

"We'll check it out, speak to the neighbours. She may simply have taken off to spend some of that money she's come into, but we need to know."

"Why? Is she part of this too?"

"I don't know, Grace, but she is missing."

"Stephen, can I have a word?" DCI Ron Green had come into the office and was staring at the board. He didn't look happy; the frown lines across his forehead were even deeper than usual. If Greco had to describe the DCI he'd say that he looked 'lived in,' certainly his face did. He was in his fifties and looked every day of it. What was left of his hair was greying and cut very short. He wasn't overweight but he did have the start of a paunch. The DCI himself put that down to too much beer.

"Brenda Hirst reported missing on Saturday, found murdered this morning on the canal bank."

"Have you given any more thought to the case we discussed on Friday?" asked Green, beckoning him away from the others.

"It would be a major investigation," Greco replied. "Currently our hands are tied with this." He looked at the board. "A murder has to take precedence. Has the other case become urgent?"

"It's causing me problems, yes," Green grimaced. "I've had orders from upstairs to get the Hussains banged to rights. They've gotten away with their scams for long enough and recently they've become far too blasé about it."

"Does it have to be us?" Greco questioned. "What about the other teams in the station?"

"Like you, busy and up to their eyes in it. But I have to do something; we're becoming a laughing stock. Most of Oldston is buying their cigarettes from one or other of their shops, not to mention the pubs."

"A raid would sort it, uniform could do that. Confiscate the tobacco and arrest the owner."

"We've tried that and got made to look a right lot of fools in court. Nazir Hussain, who owns the chain of small shops, is an old man but he has a clever team backing him up. He employs most of the other family members and they are sharp as razors, believe me. No — we need to catch them collecting the stuff from the docks."

"With respect, sir, murder has to take precedence over tobacco smuggling."

"I'm afraid it's no longer simply tobacco they're bringing into the country. Now they've moved into drugs too: heroin, crack, anything you care to mention. Members of that family make regular trips to Hull and Liverpool — several trips a week. They don't go into the docks, instead they handle the transactions at the motorway services close by."

"So why don't we just nick them there? From what you say we could set things up and catch them red-handed."

"It'd have to be a tight ship. Every time we've tried anything in the past they've got wind of it and we've been made to look silly."

Stephen Greco folded his arms thoughtfully. "Someone passing on information — someone from the station?"

"Nothing proved," Green added hastily. "But nonetheless the Hussains have an uncanny knack of staying one step ahead."

"The family would need watching, sir. It would have to be a proper job. They'd need tailing day and night, and that will take manpower we haven't got."

Green nodded and left him to it. "Perhaps a visit to one or two of their shops," he suggested on his way out, "on the pretext of warning about the illegal importation of cigarettes and alcohol. Let them know we haven't forgotten about them."

"I'll give it some thought, sir."

"Is that the dope and fags scam?" Quickenden asked, once the DCI had left the room. "I inquire because the Spinners was awash with the stuff over the weekend. You can get anything you want. One of the Hussain crew was practically handing round a menu." He chuckled.

"So what did you do about it, Sergeant?" Greco looked at him, annoyed. "You didn't buy any cigarettes off them, did you?" He was aware that his sergeant smoked.

"No, course not."

But he sounded shifty. "So, what *did* you do?"

"I warned the landlord, sir. I told him straight that he'd lose his licence if he got caught."

"But he did get caught, didn't he, by you, you idiot!"

Greco shook his head and went to his desk to prepare for the team briefing he would hold shortly. He'd have to keep an eye on Quickenden. The DS obviously wasn't sure on which side of the fence he belonged.

Chapter 4

"Sorry about the wait, Rose," the man said, pulling away the blanket that covered her naked body. "I had to do Brenda first. I'm sure you understand. She's been a right pain in the arse recently, heartless bitch. So I must admit I found doing her very satisfying indeed."

The woman wriggled and tried to scream but she couldn't. She was strapped down tight, lying on her back on a lumpy old sofa, and gagged. She felt sick. She was hungry and cold. The mad bastard hadn't even given her a drink of water.

"Making you wait does have its advantages though, Rose. It gave me time to do my research. You want me to make this good, don't you?" He smiled. "Of course it doesn't help me being so ignorant about anatomy. If I knew that it'd give me more scope, but as it is I'm forced to research everything I want to do. I hate those huge medical textbooks, don't you? All that jargon and those Latin names, confuses me no end. It'd help if I didn't have a head full of fairies, wouldn't it, Rose?" He laughed.

She mumbled incoherently behind the gag. Anatomy? Brenda? What in hell's name was he talking about?

"There was a lot of blood when I did Brenda, Rose," he told her, pulling a face. "It was her head. I hit her too hard, smashed her skull with a baseball bat, poor bitch." He shuddered. "Cracked like an egg and bled like a pig she did." He paused, closed his eyes and smiled. "But that's all done with now. Brenda is no more and we can have some fun."

Rose gave a strangled scream. She'd no idea who he was talking about or what was going on. Why was he telling her this, what did he expect her to do?

"You were always the one I really wanted, Rose. Brenda was a sort of practice run," he admitted. "You do believe me, don't you? You've been on my mind for a long time. The one thing I will say about Brenda, she had lovely brown eyes. When I took them out I placed them in a little jewellery box and put them in the fridge at home. Now they've taken on a delightful frosty glaze, I hope yours look as pretty."

Rose bucked against the ties, but it was no use, she was strapped down tight. He was mad, he had to be. She'd no idea who he was talking about — Brenda, who was Brenda?

"To begin with, I wanted your heart. But I've decided hearts are out, too much blood. I want to, I really do. I want to look at your heart, Rose. I want to see if it's as black as I suspect it is. But it would be risky. I'd only have to nick the aorta and it'd all go horribly wrong. You see I want you to stick around for a while. I want to see you suffer. I want that a lot, Rose," he said, leaning in close and mouthing the words quietly. "But first I thought we could get to know each other. What d'you say?"

Rose was petrified. She was shaking so hard that her teeth were chattering. Her empty stomach was churning over as she felt his hands on her body. His fingers slowly traced two lines on her belly — one vertical, one horizontal.

"I've thought about this and I think I've worked it out." He smiled down at her. "Evisceration is the way to go, plenty of guts but not much blood. I'll take your bowel a bit at a time; ease it slowly from your body without cutting into it, a bit like a hernia. I've read that the bowel is yards long, Rose; imagine that. I might hang it up there from a hook," he said, pointing to the sturdy metal beams supporting the ceiling. "You can lie here and watch your small intestine slowly shrivel. Fancy that, do you, Rose?"

* * *

The team sat around the table in the centre of the office. Greco had prepared a sheet for each of them containing the little information they had so far.

"Brenda Hirst, found dead on canal bank this morning. We have no motive for the killing," he began. "According to her husband she led a simple, blameless life, but not according to her manager at Webb's," he told them, passing the sheets around. "According to her, Brenda was having an affair. So our first problem is that we've been given two entirely different pictures of her life. We need to know which is correct. If she was having an affair, we need to know who with. Grace, go back to Webb's Travel and take statements from the staff. Ask if anyone knows or even suspects who the boyfriend is. Despite what Caroline Dulwich thinks, she might have confided in someone. Be honest with them — she was murdered, don't dress it up, but don't mention the eyes. Tell them it was a particularly nasty and violent end that she met."

Grace had been taking notes, which was good, but on the other hand, she kept checking the office clock. It was three thirty — it would be the child. Greco knew that she sometimes had a problem with care. It was a shame. Without that burden, she'd have had the makings of a good detective. "Ask if anyone saw who she was waving to on Saturday after work. If it was a lift, did anyone see who picked her up?"

"Georgina, get onto Brenda Hirst's service provider and ask for a list of calls made and received over the last fortnight. Craig, I want to know much more about Rose Donnelly's life. Her friends, any family and where she spends her time. She's missing, there may be nothing in it but the informant wouldn't leave a name and that is always suspicious. She's recently come into money. Who knew about it? When Georgina has the phone information, she'll help you."

He looked at Quickenden. He had his head in his palm and was smiling and tapping away — had he heard anything he'd said? Was he even interested?

"Sergeant, you're with me," he barked at him. For now he daren't let him loose on his own. "We'll revisit Jack Hirst and then the Duggan Centre. That pathologist must know something more by now."

"What about the Hussains and the cigarette thing?" Quickenden asked.

"Drop that for now. We'll look at it again when we've got more time. But if you see any sort of contraband or drugs changing hands in the pubs, you bring the perpetrators in — understand?"

Quickenden nodded.

"I'm sorry people but it's going to be a late one. Arrange what you have to with your families and get something to eat. We'll catch up with what we've got later."

"Where to first, sir?" Quickenden asked.

"I knew you weren't listening, Sergeant. Get your stuff, we'll go and have another chat to Jack Hirst."

* * *

"He's not in, sir," Quickenden said, rubbing his knuckles. "I've practically knocked the door down but no one's answering."

"I thought we were sending a PC round to stay with him." Greco got on the phone and rang the nick. He was annoyed — why didn't his colleagues do what he told them? He hadn't wanted Hirst left alone, for valid reasons. He wasn't completely satisfied that he'd had nothing to do with his wife's murder for a start. "Apparently he cancelled, said he'd be fine."

"So what's he up to?"

At that moment Greco's mobile rang again. He stood silently listening and then gestured to the car. "Do you know where Reader's Garage is?"

"Alex Reader — the car sales guy, local lad made good; yep, it's on the High Street."

"We need to get there fast. It looks like Hirst is trying to smash the place up."

"In that case, we may have found the boyfriend, sir," Quickenden joked. "Must say I'm surprised. Alex Reader is something of a player, not the type to go for a woman like Brenda."

"So what type does he go for? Tell me about him — everything you know."

"Usually lookers, blonde and young. He's the big-headed type, self-made. He does have a wife, though, and a son. They live in glorious splendour somewhere Leesworth way. He sells cars, the posh end, and recently he's specialised in classic sports models."

"Is he a similar age to Brenda Hirst?"

"I suppose he must be, sir; like Brenda he's lived around here all his life until recently, so they could know each other from way back."

* * *

Quickenden needed a few minutes to ring Les at the Spinners. There was another card game on tonight. Geegee and the lads would expect him to turn up but it was looking highly likely he wouldn't make it. Greco was a pain. He was so full on and there wasn't a laugh in him.

He'd no idea what sort of a private life he had, but heaven help any woman he had waiting at home for him.

They pulled up into the shopper's car park. Reader's Car Sales was just across the road. It looked quiet enough, until a woman rushed out of the main entrance, screaming blue murder.

"Get uniform down here," Greco told him, already out of the car.

Quickenden hung back as the boss started for the showroom. Seconds later he was on his phone but not to the nick.

"Les," he began, "I won't be in till much later. It's too busy at work and I can't get away."

"You're part of the circle, mate. Geegee won't like it. You took a packet off him Friday night."

"A packet? It was only a ton!" the sergeant exclaimed. "You know as well as I do that Geegee can afford it."

"He still won't like it; he'll think you're taking the piss. You know what he's like. Cop or no cop, he doesn't like being taken for a mug."

"Look, tell him I'll try and get there, if not it'll have to be tomorrow. That's the best I can do."

Bloody Grady Gibbs, or 'Geegee' as he was more widely known, who did he think he was? Mind you Quickenden didn't want to cross him. He was a mad bastard and not frightened of taking risks. Being a cop wouldn't be any protection if Geegee took against him. Greco would have a fit if he knew he was mixing with the likes of him. But despite everything, Quickenden liked him. The guy was everything that was wrong with Oldston and it made him a right laugh.

Greco was looking over. He had that face on. The sergeant groaned; was there no peace? He took out his phone again and rang the station for back-up.

Chapter 5

"You do as you're told, nothing more. You can follow simple instructions, can't you, Daz?" The older man gave Darren Hopper a warning look. "Because if you can't, and you let me down . . ." He smiled and cuffed the lad's chin lightly. "Let me down and things won't go well for you. You understand what I'm saying, Daz?"

Darren Hopper understood alright. Normally he wouldn't go anywhere near Geegee. The man wasn't wired right — a proper nutjob is what Tanweer had said about him. But things being as they were, what choice did he have?

Geegee had collared him on Oldston High Street. He'd dragged him down an alleyway and told him he had a job for him. You didn't refuse Geegee; like he'd said, things could go hellishly wrong if you did.

The man was a lot older than Daz. It was difficult to pin an age on him, but if Daz had to guess, he'd say about mid-forties. His face was heavily lined, almost wizened and he always looked untidy. Today he was sporting at least two days' growth on his face and he had his long hair tied in a ponytail. Drink, drugs and being half-starved for most of his youth had taken its toll. Nowadays Geegee could afford whatever he wanted but he was an odd sort. He was either out doing business or glued to a computer in the poky flat he lived in. He certainly didn't live the lifestyle that went with the money he must be raking in from all his scams. The drug dealing alone must bring in a fortune, but you'd never guess it from looking at him.

"I want you to get that Asian mate of yours to go with you," he said, making it sound more like a threat than a suggestion. "There's a ton in it for both of you."

Daz doubted that Tanweer Hussain would be up for it. There was bad blood between Tan's family and Geegee. They didn't approve of Tanweer mixing with him, never mind with the likes of Grady Gibbs. But the dosh would help.

"What's the catch?" Daz asked nervously. There was bound to be one. Nothing was ever straightforward where Geegee was concerned.

"No catch — it's a simple enough job. Do you want it or not?"

"When do we get paid?"

"Fifty now for each of you, and fifty when the job's done."

Daz looked at the man. Could he trust him? This wasn't how Geegee usually operated. He got people to do his bidding by intimidation not money. So what made this job so different? But Geegee wasn't in the mood for answering questions, and Daz needed the cash, so what choice did he have?

"Okay, you're on — what do you want us to do?"

Geegee fished in his pocket and pulled out a wad of notes. He carefully counted out one hundred pounds and handed it to Daz along with an envelope.

"Tickets for a little coach trip you're both going on," he told him with a smirk. "Follow the instructions to the letter, and don't mess up. Come round to my place tonight, after dark, and I'll give you your luggage."

Daz scratched his head. Coach trip, what was that all about? Geegee looked even shiftier than normal.

"Why don't we just take our own luggage?" Daz asked.

"Because you'll take what I give you, that's why."

Daz shuffled his feet. He was nervous, uncomfortable, this wasn't good. It must be a delivery of some sort, possibly drugs. But if that was the case, why wasn't Geegee being upfront about it? Everyone knew he ran drugs and he made no secret of it when he collared some poor sod for a drop. Something double dodgy, then, not drugs, so, what?

"Where're we going?"

"Nowhere," Geegee sneered. "You get off at the first stop — it'll be a motorway services, then you scarper. There'll be a car parked up for you. I'll give you the keys later. Most importantly, you leave your luggage in the hold of the coach, where the driver puts it when you get on, and you don't tell anyone. In fact, you don't draw attention to yourselves on the coach at all — understand?"

Daz nodded.

"Let me down and I'll do you, you and your mate — got it? And make sure the mate you take is that Asian guy you're so fond of —no one else. Don't get that wrong either."

Daz nodded. Like it not, it looked like he'd have to get Tan involved. He might not want to do Grady Gibbs's dirty work but it was better than nothing. He'd better go find Tan and tell him the good news.

* * *

"Do something about that crazy fool; he's smashing up my showroom!" Alex Reader shouted when Greco showed him his warrant card.

"Mr Hirst!" he called out to the angry man, but Hirst was so enraged he didn't seem to hear him.

"Not the Sprite!"

47

Reader darted forward and tried to wrench the office chair from Hirst's hands. Hirst had been about to lob it at the sports car.

"Do you know how much that's worth?"

"You killed her, you bastard!" Hirst flung back, trying to punch Reader in the face. He was crimson with rage. Despite Greco's attempts to intervene, Hirst lunged for Reader and on the second try managed to knock him to the ground.

"I never touched her!" Reader shrieked back, sliding along the showroom floor on his backside. "You've got this all wrong. Brenda and I were not having an affair."

"You've got her phone, so how did that happen?" Hirst demanded, kicking out with his booted foot and connecting with Reader's hip.

Quickenden arrived and hauled Hirst away, pushing him against the showroom counter. "Give it up," he warned, while Greco helped Reader to his feet.

"So how did you manage to get Mrs Hirst's phone?" the DI asked, as Reader brushed down his expensive suit.

"I don't know. She must have left it in the car."

"What car?" Greco asked.

"That frog-eyed Sprite." He nodded towards it. "The one he was about to destroy. It was on Saturday night. I gave her a lift after work. She had shopping and I was practically going past her street. She liked the car. It was no big deal. I'd been promising her a ride in it for a while."

"But that's not where you dropped her, is it?"

"No. She wanted out before we got there." He hung his head.

"Why was that?"

"We had words," he admitted, "nothing heavy but Brenda got angry and wanted out."

"So, if you weren't having an affair, what was going on?" Greco demanded.

"I'd rather not say," came the sheepish reply.

Greco was just about to tell him exactly why he should say, when Hirst wriggled out of Quickenden's grip and ran to the Sprite. Moments later he screamed.

"There's blood in the boot! What did I say? He killer her, I knew it."

"Watch him," Greco told Quickenden, going to see for himself. Right enough, the carpet covering the floor of the boot had several small bloodstains on it. "The phone, where is it now?" he demanded.

"In the office, on my desk," Reader replied. "Look I don't know how the blood got there but Brenda was fine when I left her."

"I'd like you to come down to the station with us, Mr Reader, and answer a few more questions."

Reader sighed heavily and nodded.

"Uniform have arrived, sir," Quickenden told him.

"Take Reader out and hand him over to them. We'll follow shortly."

"I'll take you home, Mr Hirst. I've got some more questions for you too."

Greco rang the Duggan Centre; he wanted the CSI people to look at the Sprite.

"Sergeant, we'll give Mr Hirst a lift home. Take him to our car and wait with him, please."

He looked at the terrified female receptionist. "I want the showroom closed and no one is to touch that car. The forensic science people will come and collect it so make sure you have the keys ready for them. Now show me to Mr Reader's office, please."

The phone was where Reader had said it was. Greco picked it up using a clean tissue and placed it in an evidence bag he took from his coat pocket.

Hirst remained stubbornly quiet during the short drive home. He looked pale, shocked by what had happened, what he'd done.

"You deliberately kept your wife's relationship with Reader from us," Greco stated, once they were inside his house. "Why would you do that?" He watched the man flop exhausted onto the sofa.

"Because I was ashamed. I'd never have believed that Brenda could do that to me."

"Did you suspect?"

Hirst inhaled deeply then nodded his head. "She was going out more, and she started having her hair done at that posh place in town."

"Dead give-away that," Quickenden muttered, rolling his eyes.

"You see the problem I have, Mr Hirst, is that your jealousy regarding Reader gives you a motive," Greco told him, ignoring his sergeant.

"I'd never hurt Brenda," he protested. "You're barking up the wrong tree there. Ask anyone; I was devoted to that woman."

"Reader denied the affair, sir," Quickenden reminded him.

"Well, he would, wouldn't he?" Hirst scoffed.

"I'm going to arrange for a uniformed officer to stay with you," Greco decided. "And the offer is not negotiable," he added.

"The Duggan Centre, sir?" Quickenden asked, once they'd dropped Hirst off.

"No. We'll let them work on the car and the phone first. We'll go back to the station and have a word with Alex Reader."

* * *

"You've got this all wrong," said Reader to the two detectives. "Anyway Brenda wasn't my type. Surely you can see that?"

"What I saw, Mr Reader, was a woman who'd been bludgeoned to death. Your type or not, I think you need to explain what was going on between the two of you."

The man fell silent for a few moments.

"We're waiting, Mr Reader."

"She didn't want anyone to know. I promised her I wouldn't say anything about it, ever." He looked into Greco's face. "I promised, Inspector, and she trusted me."

The look on Reader's face told Greco that this was a big deal for him. Breaking his promise, even one made to a woman who was now dead, wasn't something he'd do lightly.

"Promise or no promise, Brenda was murdered and we need to exclude you from our enquiries. Given the evidence we've just discovered, surely you want that too?" He gave him a few moments to think about it. "What did you promise her?" Greco persisted. "I don't think you appreciate the seriousness of this and the trouble you're in. The woman is dead. Nothing you say now can hurt her, but it could help you."

"Brenda needed money," he admitted reluctantly. "And she didn't know anyone else who could lend her the amount she wanted."

"Why would you agree to lend her money?"

"She's a friend — was a friend," he corrected himself. "We went to school together, we used to hang out. We always spoke, she'd pop in to the showroom, drool over the cars, share a joke, you know."

"What was the money for?" Quickenden asked.

More silence as Reader looked from one man to the other. "Please don't tell anyone else about this. It would hurt that fool of a husband of hers so much. Not that he deserves our protection." He paused.

"Protection from what?"

"Brenda was pregnant," he said at last, "about three months. She didn't want the baby and she was adamant about it. There was no doubt in her mind."

"And her husband — what about him?"

"She didn't tell him. Brenda wanted the money for an abortion in a private clinic."

"You know that this is easily checked, Mr Reader. There will be a post-mortem," Greco reminded him.

Reader sat back in his chair staring at his feet. What was going through his head? The mention of a PM had rattled him, Greco could see. He must be holding something back.

"It was mine," he admitted at last.

"So you were having a relationship?" Greco confirmed with a heavy sigh.

"No, not really, it was all in her head," he said.

"The pregnancy wasn't in her head."

"We had a fling, a one-night stand; she was lonely, fed up. She came round to the showroom after work and she didn't want to go home. We talked. I opened a bottle of scotch and I suppose we got a little drunk." He shrugged. "The next thing, we were . . ." He inhaled and looked away. "You know . . . at it."

"What happened after that?"

"Brenda had the wrong idea entirely. It wasn't meant to be anything serious. But she wouldn't let it go. She kept dropping in, all dressed up, and asking to go out. I told her I couldn't. My wife has had enough. I'm on a final warning as it is. If she finds out I've played away again, she'll take me for every penny."

"Do you know a woman called Rose Donnelly?" Greco asked. "Were you having an affair with her too?"

Greco saw Reader's face cloud over. It appeared he knew the name, so why not just say so? What was going through the man's mind?

"No, of course not," he said at last. "I don't know that woman."

Greco could tell from his face and demeanour that this was a lie, but he had no proof.

"I take it you are prepared to give us a DNA sample?" Greco asked.

Reader nodded.

"Arrange that and leave it on my desk, Sergeant," Greco told Quickenden. "Was it you, Mr Reader, who rang

Brenda during the day on her mobile while she was at work?"

"Yes, mostly to make an excuse as to why I couldn't see her. She wouldn't take the hint. On Saturday night when I gave her a lift home I told her straight. It had to stop. I'd had enough."

"Did things get physical? Did you hurt her?"

"No! I never touched her. She got out of the car at the bottom of Link Road and said she'd walk."

"Did you see which way she went?"

"Towards the bottom of the estate," he told them.

"Towards the canal, then," Quickenden added.

Chapter 6

Daz was jumpy. Meeting Geegee had done him no good at all. He wandered down Oldston High Street looking for his mate. He should be hanging out by the Spinners pub or in town, but he wasn't. Half an hour of searching later he finally spotted him up a side street.

"Hey, where've you been hiding, man? I've got something for you."

Tanweer Hussain smiled at his friend. He was standing with a group of Asian men. "I've been to the mosque," he said, nodding at the golden-domed building behind him. "We've been weighing up what repairs need doing."

"Sorry, mate. I'll leave you to it if you've got a lot on."

"No, it's okay but be quick cos Kashif will be out anytime."

Kashif was his older brother — a brute of a man who didn't like Daz much.

"I've done something, something stupid, and I've dragged you into it too." Daz grimaced, leading Tan out of earshot of the others.

"Dragged me into what?"

"Doing a job for Geegee, that's what." He saw his mate's face fall.

"That lunatic? You're having me on," Tan replied angrily.

"Look calm down — it's not that bad, it's easy money — a ton each." Who was he trying to kid? Any involvement with Gibbs was bad. "Forget it's for Geegee, the job's a piece of cake, and there's cash up front for us both," he said, taking the notes from his pocket. "Here, this is for you." He tried to push the notes into Tan's hands. "All we have to do is take a trip out Thursday, and it's nothing hard either. We're going on a short coach ride, one of Webb's trips." Daz grinned. "Fifty notes for now and he'll give us another fifty when we get back."

He watched Tanweer eye the money with suspicion. He needed a *yes*, he'd promised Geegee. Tanweer was a pushover in comparison to his older brother. Tan was a gentle soul who did as he was told.

"Stace'll kill you if you get mixed up with him again," Tan said, referring to Daz's girlfriend.

"Then I won't tell her. Once she's got the money in her hands, she'll not ask too many questions." Daz nodded. "And if she does, I'll tell her we're doing something for Kashif. Here, take it." He pushed the money at his friend again. "Just say you'll come with me. It's a short coach ride for an hour or so, nothing heavy."

"Where're we going?"

"We're not. We get off once it pulls in to the first services. Geegee reckons we should wear something, you know, a disguise, when we leave, so we're not picked up on the CCTV."

"So it's dodgy. Kashif won't like it. He hates the bloke. You know there's practically all-out war between them at the moment, don't ask me what about. They're both as bad as each other."

That much was true. Both men were constantly battling for supremacy in the local drug trade. If you didn't buy from one, then you bought from the other. There was no one else. Daz knew that currently Kashif had the edge and that Geegee didn't like it.

"And what if Kashif needs me for something?" Tanweer bleated.

"He doesn't own you — tell him you're busy." Daz shrugged.

"Can't you earn a crust some other way, bro? Geegee isn't good for you, he isn't good for anybody. The man's toxic."

"There's nowt out there, Tan. You haven't got a clue. Kashif keeps you sorted moneywise. Stace'll kill me if I don't get some dosh soon. She's said she'll throw me out if I don't bring home my share of what we need."

"She's someone else you shouldn't have got mixed up with. I told you at the time, but you don't listen, do you, bro? Now look where you've ended up."

"She was fucking pregnant, man. Her brothers were turning the screws. You could help me if you weren't so scared of Kashif. You could ask your uncle Naz if he'll take me on. His shops are open all the time and he's always looking for people."

Tan looked doubtful. "I'll try. I'll speak to him later, if Kashif leaves me alone."

"Try your best, mate. I need something quick, rent's due again. D'you think Naz'll bother, you know, about my record and stuff?"

"Don't tell him, bro, just don't tell him."

Darren Hopper thought about this for a second or two as he rocked on his heels. A job with Naz could be good, and Tan was right — what the old man didn't know, well, couldn't hurt, could it? Anyway, he hadn't really spent time inside, not properly. He'd been in a young offenders' unit and that didn't count. You were allowed a few mistakes, surely, growing up.

"What you up to now?" Tan asked, suddenly engrossed with his mobile phone.

"Nowt. I've been down the jobcentre but that's a waste of time. Now they want me to join some job club. They want me in every day and if I refuse . . ." He shrugged. "The bastards say they'll stop my benefit."

"Got a text off Kashif, he wants me to go with him, he's got stuff to do," Tan told his friend. "Not a word about Geegee or he'll have my guts."

At that moment an overweight Asian man with a full beard lumbered through the mosque door towards them.

"Tanweer. With me," he barked, giving Darren a filthy look. "What have I told you about hanging around with him? You've got work to do."

"Lucky sod," Daz muttered. He didn't like Tan's older brother and the feeling was mutual. Kashif was odd, secretive, and then there were the rumours. People didn't trust him, said he was a radical, an extremist and that he spent far too much time stirring up the local Asian youth. He'd taken a bunch of them to London not so long ago, to a huge rally in Hyde Park. God knows what for — some protest about injustice in some place Daz had never heard of.

"He is a very lucky boy, but does he appreciate what his family does for him?" He clapped Tan on the back. "No, he most certainly does not. Instead he does stupid things like hanging around street corners with the likes of you," Kashif Hussain said, poking Darren in the chest. "So why don't you go home to that woman of yours and leave Tanweer alone?"

"We've been hanging out since school," Daz protested. "You've never been bothered before." Then he took a step back. Kashif's eyes were wild, glittering with something Daz didn't like. There was a lot of hate in the man.

"Well, I'm bothered now," he growled. "You got no job to go to?"

"Not yet, but I'm looking," Daz replied.

"Then go down the Job Centre and look there. You're not going to find anything lurking on street corners with this idle lump, are you? Unless it's trouble you want, eh, Darren?"

"Just want to make some money, Kashif, that's all. No crime is it, wanting to feed your family? Tan said he'd have a word with your uncle for me."

"You'd do better to look somewhere else. Naz can't help." Kashif glowered at Tan.

"He's got something on this week, haven't you Daz?" Tanweer said, "so you see, he does try. It wouldn't do any harm to ask Uncle Naz, and you need drivers, you said so this morning."

Kashif shot his brother a look that was positively murderous. "Stupid fool," he rasped in his face. "That's family business. I've warned you about that slack mouth of yours. It'll get you into real trouble one of these days."

"But Daz is okay, he really is, and he can be trusted. Besides, like he says, he needs the money and he's not particular."

Daz might not like Kashif but he was curious about the man. He knew, as did most of Oldston, that Tan's family ran a racket in imported cigarettes as well as drugs. His drivers visited the docks in Liverpool or Hull on a regular basis. They'd pick up the stuff and then distribute it among dozens of shops run by family or friends. A very lucrative sideline, guessed Darren, and he would love to be in on the action.

"You talking about the ciggy run, Tan?" He smiled, nodding at Kashif with a look that said he knew all about it.

"What if he is?" Kashif sighed. "The young fool isn't involved, and you'd do well to keep that stupid mouth of yours shut." His face and those evil eyes loomed, only centimetres from Daz's. "You've no idea what catastrophes can befall someone who falls foul of our operation," he said. "So keep your nose out and don't concern yourself with our business. Do you understand?"

What Darren understood was that he had yet another dodgy bastard threatening him with God knows what. But it still didn't stop him from wanting in. "I'm the soul of discretion. Believe me, I can be trusted. I need to earn some money and I'm not too bothered what I have to do to get it."

Straight down the line. There was no way Kashif could misinterpret what he wanted now — Darren Hopper really did want in.

Daz waited while Kashif Hussain considered this. He was quiet for a few seconds before finally shaking his head decisively.

"No — no way. This is family business, family only, you understand?" Kashif said, giving Darren an evil smile. "So there is no place for a toerag like you."

* * *

"Do we say anything to her husband, sir?" Quickenden asked, after they'd let Reader go.

"Not yet. We need proof to back up what he's just told us. Once we get the DNA results on the foetus, then we'll see."

"So what now?"

"The Duggan Centre," Greco decided. "I want to know what the PM has thrown up."

"Do you want me to come?"

Quickenden really shouldn't have had to ask that.

"Better things to do, Sergeant?"

"I thought I'd pop round to the Spinners, see who's selling what and see if anyone wants to talk to me."

"I think that's very unlikely." Greco sighed. "Your time would be better spent dealing with the case in hand."

"I'm not sure if you know, but the Spinners is close to the canal. It's only a few hundred yards from where the body was found. Who knows what was seen, and folk are more likely to talk to me."

He could have something there. Greco was sick of constantly having to be on Quickenden's back. "But don't think you can swan off and do your own thing. I will expect a short report on your findings in the morning. So don't use your visit as an excuse to get bladdered again. If you come in late tomorrow morning, or smelling of booze, then you're out. Do you understand?"

He watched his sergeant squirm.

"I thought it might help, sir. If there's any talk, then I'll hear it. The place is a focal point for all the scroats in this town."

Greco wondered what that made Quickenden. He returned to the main office. It was empty. Grace Harper had left a note on his desk explaining her absence. It was written on a scrappy bit of paper and had been left under his stapler, and this fact bothered him more than what it said.

They had a difficult case on their hands and his team were all lightweights. He had expected more from Quickenden. The DCI had told him that the sergeant was on a final warning. He needed to sharpen up his act and fast.

Grace Harper was more difficult to deal with. If it was possible to sweep away all the family stuff, then she did have the makings of a good detective. They bothered him: Quickenden, Grace and to a certain extent Craig Merrick too.

As he rearranged the items on the desktop, lining everything up an exact distance apart, he knew he was in trouble again. His obsession with neatness and cleanliness, if left unchecked, could take over his life and leave him precious little time for anything else. He resolved to register with a local GP and get some help.

He looked up at the clock: six thirty. Craig Merrick entered the office with a pile of files under his arm.

"Thought I catch up with this little lot while it was quiet," he explained.

"Don't apologise to me for working hard, but if that's all getting a bit boring, perhaps you fancy a trip to the Duggan Centre?"

Merrick looked up and nodded.

"You drive and then you can drop me off at home when we've finished."

"Earlier I was looking at the last calls made to and from Brenda Hirst's phone," he told the DI. "She got a call, sir, from an unknown user. It's the last one logged. She spoke to someone for about three minutes."

"Can we find out who it was?"

"Probably, but I don't have the right access to what I need, to do that.

"In that case it needs to go to the Duggan. It could be an important break. Good work."

"Have I got time to grab a sandwich before we leave, sir?"

"Okay — about fifteen minutes," Greco told him.

The DI took the Donnelly file from his desk.

"I've got another one for you," said DCI Green, coming into the office. "Central has passed me the tobacco scam information. Thought I'd let you have a look, and if the murder investigation starts to drag, then you could consider giving it some time."

"It's still early days — the investigation has a way to go."

"And it needs the entire team?"

Greco nodded back.

"I know it's not what you want to hear but watch the budget — overtime particularly. Pathology and forensic science are bound to cost more now that it's moved to the new facility."

"DC Merrick and I are off there now, sir. We need to know what the PM has thrown up, if anything. I've met

Doctor Barrington but who've they put at the helm for forensic science?"

"Doctor Julian Batho," he replied, "Professor Batho now, since the move.

"I've met him. He's good, but the post of professor?"

"The department at the cottage hospital in Leesdon closed. Doctor Hoyle semi-retired, Batho decided to leave, applied to the Duggan and got a giant leg-up. Is he someone we can work with?"

"I met him when I was involved with a case in Leesdon. I found him quite . . . challenging. He doesn't give much away. He's difficult to read."

Greco watched the DCI smile. He knew what he'd be thinking — pot, kettle, black and all that.

"How are you getting on with the team, Stephen?" he asked, before Greco could add anything else.

Now they were getting to it.

"It's going to be hard work, sir. I hope they've got it in them to become a good bunch, but at present it's touch and go." It was no use pretending. The team was a mess, and it wasn't his fault, it was a mess he'd inherited. "Quickenden is the worst; DC Harper could do with bucking her ideas up, and Craig Merrick needs to prove he's back on the job. I read the report. I'm surprised he wasn't sacked. He was mixed up with a known criminal. Had there been any proof that he'd taken a bribe then that would have been it."

"There was none, not that could be found anyway, so go easy," Green suggested. "He's young and got in too deep. His rationale was to infiltrate a group of thugs running the take-away on Link Road, but he came unstuck. In my opinion, for what it's worth, I think they set him up. They spun him a load of lies and Merrick fell for it."

"He's a detective, he should know better. That isn't how we get things done." He shook his head. "Quickenden's another one. He's gone off early to spend time in that dive of a pub — the Spinners. He reckons he can get a lead on the tobacco scam and the murder by talking to folk in there. But they won't give anything away, not to a cop."

"That's where you're wrong, Stephen," Green said. "Merrick, no — but Quickenden is one of them, well, was one of them before he saw the light. He grew up around here, they know him. He's the archetypal bad boy made good."

"That's a matter of opinion, sir. He's still got a lot to learn."

"Try and go easy. They worked for Leighton, your predecessor, for a while and they liked him. I want you all to get along. I know Quickenden's history isn't good but, given a chance, DC Harper does try hard. If you are to succeed you need their goodwill and support. You're their DI but even you can't operate alone," he warned. "You are okay here, aren't you? Not regretting the move?"

"I'm not here out of choice if that's what you mean," Greco admitted. "It's where I need to be because of my daughter. I made that clear at the interview. But things are smoother now. Me and Suzy have a routine that works and Matilda has settled down fine. As for the job I've no complaints — crime's crime anywhere. It suits me to be busy and there's work here in abundance."

Green shook his head. "Too much bloody work if you ask me. Take my advice, get yourself a life outside of this place. You can't put work above everything else, Stephen. It does no one any good and your team need you to be on top form."

"Pep talk over, sir." He'd had enough. He had things to do.

"When we're talking privately, call me Colin." The DCI smiled. "This *yes sir, no sir* stuff has its place but I'd like us to get on aside from that."

Greco nodded. Well, if that's what he wanted. The others in his team all used first names and even nicknames: Quickenden was Speedy and he'd heard Georgina called

George on more than one occasion. It wasn't something he was comfortable with but on reflection it was a habit he too was falling into. He'd see how things went.

Chapter 7

The Duggan Centre was a purpose built pathology and forensic science lab on the business park along the Manchester bypass. It offered its diverse facilities far and wide. All the CID in the surrounding areas used it, as the move for centralisation gained momentum. It specialised in DNA analysis and was pioneering the newest techniques.

"Doctor Barrington," Greco said to the woman on reception, as he and Merrick showed their IDs.

She rang through to the labs, then pointed down the corridor. "Doctor Barrington is in post-mortem room three," she told them.

"Attended many of these?" he asked Merrick as they went.

The DC shook his head and shivered. "Hate them — I've only ever seen two done and they scared the sh . . . well, they scared me."

"I'm not too keen myself," Greco replied. "It's not the dead, so much as all the emotion that goes with the loss."

Merrick shot him a look and Greco smiled back. "Didn't have me down as being into empathy, did you?

I'm not a heartless man, Constable, but it's better for your own sanity if you can maintain a certain detachment."

"Inspector Greco!" The pathologist greeted them as they entered the room.

In this environment Natasha Barrington looked completely different — lack of white coverall, Greco decided. She was younger than he'd thought earlier, mid-thirties. She had a pretty face with a smattering of freckles. The hair he'd thought was dark was actually a deep shade of auburn bobbing on her shoulders. His daughter, Matilda, had freckles. He smiled at the thought.

"You're leaving?" She had her coat on and was busy organising the contents of her briefcase.

"You policemen, never know when to call it a day. Some of us have a life, Inspector. I recommend it, keeps you sane."

"The body from this morning — I have a few questions."

She went to her computer and brought up a file. "Brenda Hirst. It's as I thought: blow to the head with something wooden, no sharp edges but with a force hard enough to leave splinters in the wound. Under the microscope we could see that some of the splinters had a smooth edge on one side."

"A baseball bat," Merrick suggested.

"That would do it, that or something similar, and wielded by someone strong because it had force behind it. Her skull was shattered so badly that a sliver of bone entered the Medulla Oblongata. Death would have been instant. But not content with that, your killer then stamped on her head leaving the boot imprint we saw this morning."

"Was she pregnant?" Greco asked.

"Yes, I was just coming to that, about three months. I'll print the report out for you," she said.

"Was there any evidence of sexual assault prior to her death?"

"No, I found nothing untoward."

"Would you arrange for the DNA of the foetus to be matched against this?" He handed her the saliva sample taken from Reader.

"Professor Batho will do that for you. I believe he has one or two other things he'd like to discuss."

"Is he still here?"

Natasha Barrington rolled her eyes and grinned. "Unlike me he practically lives here. This job is obviously what the man was waiting for." She picked up the phone and tapped in an extension number. "But not tonight, it seems. I'm afraid he must have gone."

"I'll ring him tomorrow."

"You're not from this area, are you?" She smiled, handing him the printed Brenda Hirst file. "It's the accent."

"I transferred from East Anglia — a personal matter." He didn't want to elaborate. It was his private life and that wasn't for discussing with strangers, no matter how attractive. Apart from which, Merrick had large ears and would no doubt relate anything he said back to the team.

"Must be very different from what you were used to. Life's harder up here, well, it is in Oldston. Substance abuse is a major killer. You'd be surprised how much death we see due to drugs and drink."

"I think not, we had that in Norfolk too," he said. "We also have a large number of homeless people. The seaside towns are the worst."

"Life can be tragic sometimes, Inspector. I never fail to be touched by the waste. Take your woman today, for example. She was still young, in her forties, and had everything to live for. And she was pregnant, how sad is that?"

"We do what we can. If people stay within the boundaries, it helps."

"But they don't, and who can blame them? There are no jobs unless you want to stack shelves for minimum wage or work your socks off in some back-street café. People live hand to mouth and do what they can. Unfortunately that often means crime. I'm afraid the lifestyle lived by many around here has consequences."

Most pathologists he'd met maintained an aloof detachment from their work. Like him, they'd cultivated it. They had to; it was a job that could easily get you down.

"Perhaps I should show you around the place. Take you down the odd backstreet after dark; let you experience Oldston at its worst. Show you what we're all up against."

Greco couldn't tell if the woman was serious or not. Did she mean it exactly as she'd said or was it a lead up to asking him out for a drink? He was confused. He couldn't read women. It was a problem he'd had with Suzy. Merrick smirking away beside him didn't help.

"I think I've seen that already, this morning," he reminded her.

"Okay, in that case I could show you the prettier spots. A walk in the hills perhaps?"

She wasn't giving up. "When things aren't so busy," he agreed politely.

"You should take me up on the offer. We could round the evening off with a drink. It'd do you good," she added as she made for her car. "Do feel free to ask about anything you find puzzling."

So it was a chat up line — of sorts.

"I think she likes you, sir." Merrick was still smirking.

"Just being polite, Constable, that was all," he told him firmly.

* * *

"You take these two bags, one each. They're both locked and you don't interfere with them in any way, got it?"

Grady Gibbs had a cigarette hanging out of his mouth and he smelled of booze. Daz nodded. The man was a dangerous moron. He wouldn't have gone anywhere near him if he hadn't needed the money. He sniffed; the place smelled foul. Gibbs lived in a flat on Link Road, on the estate, and he was no housekeeper. Dirty pots were piled high in the kitchen sink and the furniture was covered in dog hairs from the vicious-looking mutt that lived with him. The only item that looked new and cared for was the expensive looking laptop he had on a desk in the centre of the room.

"When do we get the rest of the cash?"

"Come round Thursday night when you're done, I'll pay you then."

"Who's that?" Daz asked, looking at a man's face that suddenly appeared on the laptop screen. Daz didn't know the man, but he'd seen him somewhere before. He was young, with fair hair and odd-looking eyes. Daz bent forward and looked a little closer. His eyes were different colours: one blue, one brown.

"Friend of mine, and I wouldn't look too closely if I was you. If he thought you could recognise him again, then he'd kill you." Geegee grinned.

Geegee turned, keyed in a few letters and then the screen went blank.

"Skype your mates, do you?"

"He's not a mate and that's not Skype."

"Yep, it is. I've used it myself."

Geegee laughed and shook his head. "We don't use the same stuff as you, shit brain. We work exclusively on the dark net — best way with contacts like mine."

Dark net — what in hell's name was that? And what did he mean by *we*?

"If you want stuff, special stuff that you don't want anybody to trace, then it's the only way," he explained.

Daz shrugged. He'd no idea what he was on about. "You talking about dope?"

"No, I'm talking about guns — something clean. And not a word," he said, grabbing Daz by the throat. "Tell tales out of school and I'll cut your tongue out and make you eat it."

Daz was shaking. Geegee would too — that sounded exactly like something he would do.

"All the instructions are on the ticket in the envelope I gave you. Take those bags and these car keys. It's an old Ford parked on the south car park. The registration is on the key fob. Here are your disguises," he said, passing him a holdall. "Don't be late, and for fuck's sake don't miss the coach. You leave at the first motorway services. You whip on the disguises and you scarper. That's all you have to do. Simple isn't it?"

Daz nodded but his eyes were constantly being drawn back to the laptop. It had sprung to life again and that same man seemed to be watching them. Who was he and what the hell was Geegee up to?

"Get out and don't let me down," the thug warned, holding the front door open for him.

* * *

It had gone nine when Quickenden got to the Spinners. He'd left the nick and gone home, falling asleep on his sofa. A quick shower and a change of clothes and he was ready to go again.

"Thought I'd never get away," Craig Merrick said, coming up behind him with a pint in his hand. "Had to go to the bloody morgue with Greco, gave me the creeps, but she's nice, that pathologist they've got. I don't understand how it works but she seems to like the boss," Merrick said, with a laugh.

"You lads in?" A gruff voice interrupted.

It was Geegee. He was seated at a window table with three others and all of them were chain smoking.

"How does he get away with doing that in here?"

"Because no one would dare tackle him about it, that's why," Quickenden replied. "And don't you say anything either. When we're with this lot, we're not cops, we're one of the boys, got it?"

Jed Quickenden knew that Merrick looked up to him. Daft bugger — he should have chosen someone with more respect for the job. "I took Geegee for a ton last night — he's losing his touch. But take it easy, don't bet more that you can afford and don't get dragged into anything heavy."

Merrick nodded.

"Nice to meet you again." Geegee grinned at Merrick. "You're that naughty boy who took Don's cash in return for keeping his gob shut." He laughed when he saw Merrick's face fall. "Like your style, lad. Just a shame you got busted." Now they all laughed. "But it won't stop us taking all that hard-earned cash off you," he sniggered to his cronies. "Take a pew, get comfy, it's going to be a long night."

Quickenden went to the bar to get some drinks and beckoned Merrick to follow. "Give us a hand," he told him. "Don't take any notice. Let Geegee think what he likes, it makes you acceptable in his eyes," he reassured him. "Watch a couple of hands, then get in there. This lot are not as good as they think they are. There's money to be made, believe me."

They carried the drinks back to the table and sat down. Both men watched closely as Geegee shuffled the cards and dealt.

"You in, lad?" he asked Merrick.

Quickenden nudged his knee under the table and Merrick shook his head.

The table fell silent as each of the players studied their hand.

"I'm out." Geegee tossed his cards onto the table and took a swig of his beer.

Quickenden studied his hand carefully. Two of the others had followed Geegee, so it was just him and a scruffy bugger called Pete. "Raise you twenty," Quickenden said, as straight-faced as he could manage.

"Raise you right back, copper," Pete said, defiantly slapping a twenty, followed by a tenner onto the table.

"Last of the big hitters, our Pete," Geegee said, clapping him on the back.

"Room for one more?" A woman approached the table and wriggled in beside Geegee. "You said you'd come round. I waited for you," she pouted petulantly at him. "See I'm wearing it, fits nice." She showed off a gold wristwatch to the card players. "You lot think he's nothing but a rough bastard but he can show a lady a good time when he's in the mood." She grinned.

Quickenden checked out the watch and smiled. Lady. She was nothing but a good lay.

"Go amuse yourself, Lily," said Geegee.

Quickenden watched Geegee frown. Was it the interruption or the fact she'd flashed the watch? He wondered if it was stolen.

"Back to the game, lads. The silly bitch can amuse herself for a bit," he said, handing her a tenner.

"Raise you fifty." Underneath his cool exterior Quickenden was a bag of nerves. There was quite an amount on the table now and he intended it should end up in his pocket, but he had to stay focused.

"Cover that and raise you ten more."

Quickenden licked his lips, his eyes flicking back to the cards in his hand.

"Raise you—"

"Okay, I'm done, I'm folding," Pete said, suddenly throwing his cards onto the pile on the table.

Quickenden smirked and gathered up the cash. Like sweets from a baby. He was loving this.

The lads cheered and one of them got up to get more beer.

"We could make this more interesting," Geegee suggested, with a smile that showed off his gappy teeth.

Merrick felt his stomach flip. He didn't feel at all comfortable with this crew.

"A ton minimum," he said. "In or out, make your minds up, then let's see the colour of your money. What's it to be, copper?"

Quickenden watched Merrick shake his head.

"What the hell's he come for if not to play?" Geegee complained.

"Never mind him. I'm in," the sergeant said, counting his notes.

"Lads?"

Three of them nodded but Pete cried off, going to the bar and sliding up next to Lily instead.

And so it began. Fifteen minutes later Quickenden was still about even. He'd lost a couple of games and won one. But the others were getting bored. If Geegee didn't win, then the sergeant did and that wasn't what they'd come for.

"Just you and me, then." Geegee grinned again. "How about one last game — winner takes all. We'll up the stakes and have some fun.

Quickenden was high on drink and the buzz of gambling. He nodded. He felt Merrick knock his arm, but he didn't even look round.

Geegee took a deck of fresh cards and handed them to Merrick to shuffle. "Make it fair." He pulled on his cigarette and coughed. "You deal," he said to Quickenden.

He felt Merrick nudge him again — what was his problem? At this rate he'd lose his concentration, no good with so much money at stake.

"A ton." Geegee fanned out the notes, wafted them in Quickenden's face and stuck them on the table.

"See you and raise another ton."

You could cut the atmosphere in the Spinners with a knife. Everyone had fallen silent as they watched this little drama play out.

There was five hundred in the pot, but still Geegee wouldn't give up. No one breathed as his opponent examined his cards. "Five ton more." He grinned. "Match it or fold."

"I'll match that and raise you a grand." The words were out before Quickenden could stop them.

There were gasps.

Quickenden studied his hand. He had two pairs. Was it enough? "Let's see you, brave boy," he taunted.

"Not just yet." Geegee took a swig of beer and dug in his pocket, taking out another wad of notes. "Let's see what you're really made of, copper."

The first flutter of nerves hit the sergeant's stomach. The bastard couldn't have a better hand than him — could he? He had to be bluffing.

"I'll put in another two grand. Match it or fold."

"Okay, you're on." It was sheer bravado. There was no way he could afford this. "But I don't carry that much cash on me. I'll have to do an IOU."

More silence, as the pub waited for Geegee's reaction. He didn't normally give credit and he didn't like folk trying it on.

But this time it would be different.

"Okay, copper — write your little IOU. It'll do for me."

Quickenden could barely write he was so nervous. He scribbled on a page from his notebook, ripped it out and put it in the pot. "It's for three grand, so I'll see you."

"Indulge me." Geegee grinned. "You go first."

Why not? Quickenden was convinced he had the better hand. "A pair of twos," he said cockily, spreading the cards on the table. He watched Geegee's face fall. Relief; it was going to be okay — he had him.

"Pity." Geegee sniffed. "Clever bugger." He tilted his head. "Thought you had me screwed," he said at last. Then he smiled and spread his hand out on the table for all to see. "Only kidding," he grinned, "a full house!" He bowed and the pub cheered. "My pot, I believe."

Quickenden wanted to throw up. He couldn't believe what he'd just done. The stupidity of his actions hit him like a thunderbolt. What had possessed him? Greed, that's what, pure greed.

"You'll honour the IOU tomorrow." Geegee pointed a finger at the sergeant, "because if you don't, I'll get angry, and we don't want that, do we?"

God, he was in trouble now. Quickenden looked around for Merrick. Why hadn't the fool stopped him?

Chapter 8

"I know fear, Rose," he said to the woman. "In fact I'm something of an expert. I can sense it, see it even. It's in the sweat, it's on the face and it's in the eyes. It's always in the eyes," he told her. "That's why I like them so much. They remind me of the kill."

He was humming. A tuneless monotone filled the air as he arranged and rearranged the surgical instruments on the trolley by the sofa she lay on. He needed to get it right. He wanted everything perfect.

The one he'd done before had been satisfying, up to a point, but Rose would be the best. And because she was so special he'd gone to extra trouble, spent money on new instruments and chosen them carefully. He wanted to do particular things, examine parts of her anatomy he hadn't been able to with the other one.

Rose would wake up soon. He'd drugged her but the effect wouldn't last for long. It would be better once she became conscious and aware of her fate. She'd been on his list for long enough and he'd been patient. He'd hoped she'd get it; see the wrong she'd done — but that was unlikely. She had no conscience. So he was doing the world a favour. Rose was not a nice woman. She deserved everything that was coming to her.

Ironically, she trusted him and that made it easy. But he shouldn't be complacent. Murder wasn't easy, not if it was done properly. There was all the planning, the waiting and watching, and finally — the best bit — the taking. One slip and it could all go horribly wrong. But it hadn't; it had gone like clockwork and now he had her. He was excited, this one was so special. This time he was going to relax and have a little fun.

"There's fear in your eyes, Rose." He patted her arm reassuringly, as she slowly became conscious again. "But you shouldn't worry, you won't feel a thing, see." He dragged the tip of a knife blade across her belly. He was right: she didn't even flinch, she felt nothing. "A few more minutes and the first bit will be over. Good, eh, Rose?"

The humming had stopped. The only sound now was the ominous clatter of stainless steel on metal as he moved the instruments around. There was a degree of irritation in those movements, his confidence was ebbing away. Why couldn't he get it right? He wanted them laid out in order, but he was confused; did he have everything? He had two scalpels, a retractor, and a costotome, which was a specialised rib cutter. But if he went after her bowel, then he wouldn't need that.

He picked up the instrument, turning it around in his hands, testing it. It had two levers, the first one, he decided, must be for grasping the rib and the second one for cutting. What fascinating stuff doctors got to use. What fun they must have applying all that learning to the practical side of surgery. He put it on the shelf underneath, out of the way. He'd use that another time.

He ran his fingers lovingly over everything again, as if they were his most treasured possessions. He should make a start; he didn't have much time. He also had three kidney dishes and a potato peeler from the kitchen — perhaps not strictly kosher, but perfect, he'd found, for doing the final bit.

He smiled at her. She couldn't smile back, she was gagged as well as tied down. But her eyes were open, terrified eyes wildly scanning their surroundings, searching for an answer, searching for a way out of this.

He chuckled. He couldn't help it — it was the nerves. He was overexcited. Why was he like this, why couldn't he stay cool, in charge, like the surgeons did?

"You won't feel a thing, Rose," he told her again, trying to sound professional. "I've been kind, I've numbed the area, you know, like at the dentist."

He ran his fingers over her naked torso just to make sure. He frowned — people were so inconsiderate when it came to their bodies. She was overweight, not terribly so, but enough to make her abdomen flop, a bit like jelly. He could fix that. He could take out all that ugly fat, tighten her up, and make her firm again, but what would be the point? She'd never know.

"I almost didn't, you know, deaden the area, I mean. I wanted to punish you, Rose. There have been times when I've wanted that real bad." He smiled grimly. "You have a talent for annoying people. I bet you didn't know that, did you? You certainly annoy me."

She looked up into his face. She couldn't reply but her eyes said it all. They might be frightened eyes, but they were cold. She didn't have a clue how much she upset people, how much people suffered because of her actions — particularly him, heartless cow. But those eyes wouldn't watch him for much longer. Soon they'd be still, lifeless — like the other eyes he prized so much.

"It's getting late — I have things to do. As much as I'm enjoying this I must get on. You understand, don't you Rose?"

There was no reply, of course.

He surveyed the expanse of naked flesh laid out in front of him — he found her repulsive. He carefully positioned the blade just below her navel.

"Can you feel that, Rose?" As if he cared.

No response — stupid bitch!

The knife was sharp, small and easy to handle. He gave his victim a last look of contempt as he made that first incision. He went in deep — pausing momentarily, savouring the moment. He watched transfixed as the fresh blood pooled on the bench as it ran off her body. His hands were shaking. He loved the cutting, but he didn't love the blood so much. He slid the scalpel the length of her abdomen, making one long, straight sweep all the way down to her pubic bone.

He stood back, high on excitement. It was almost orgasmic. The wound was bleeding profusely and gaped open. It formed an ugly, livid gash down her torso.

He used the retractors to hold back the edges of the wound. He'd cut right through the mesentery, more by accident than design. He could see her intestines glistening pink and healthy inside her belly. He tentatively put his gloved index finger underneath a loop of small bowel and gently eased it out.

Had the painkiller worked or could she feel it? He looked into her eyes. He eased out a little more. "I've done it, Rose. Your innards are in my hands."

In a mute frenzy of pain and fear, she lost consciousness.

* * *

When Greco had moved to Oldston he'd bought an apartment in a small block on a newly built estate in what was allegedly the upmarket area. It was modern, easy to keep clean and there was no gardening to do. All that was taken care of by the service charge he paid. The place was spotless and not a thing was out of place. He'd furnished it simply, items with clean lines and not much in the way of ornaments or personal things.

A stranger looking at the place might be forgiven for thinking this was the show flat, for it gave away nothing about the owner. But then that was how he liked things and he hadn't decided whether he was staying yet. Life here was hard and he wasn't sure he liked it.

In one corner of the sitting room he had a desk with his laptop on it. He put down the three files in a neat pile. A little light reading for after he'd eaten — hardly that, he reminded himself. His current caseload consisted of a tobacco scam, a murder and a missing woman. He decided to check his email before he got stuck in. He lifted the laptop lid and clicked on the icon. Advertising rubbish, a ramble from his cousin in Canada and one from a man called *Arturo Greco*. This was the one he'd been waiting for. He clicked and read through the text, the sum of which was that the man couldn't offer much help. Greco cursed. Another brick wall!

Greco's passion, apart from his job, was family history. It was born out of his unusual surname and the desire to know where it had come from. He had hoped that Arturo could help. He lived in Milan and they shared a common ancestry. From the nineteenth century it was true, but you never knew what documents families kept from the past. Greco's own great, great grandfather, Lorenzo Greco, had left Italy because of some scandal or other and had settled in Buckinghamshire. He could find precious little about the man's birth or his parents, but it was a quest that served to fill the little time he had left from working or being with his daughter.

An appetising smell wafted through from the kitchen. Greco had put the slow cooker on that morning with a beef stew in it. It was probably ready by now. He didn't eat much when he was working. He'd pack a couple of sandwiches and a piece of fruit before he left and that was usually enough for the day. But now it was late and he was hungry.

He was about to dish up when the doorbell rang. He wasn't expecting visitors. He didn't know anyone in Oldston, and no one at the station knew where he lived, except for the DCI. If it was someone selling stuff, then he'd send them away with a flea in their ear. But it wasn't. At the door stood his ex-wife Suzy and their daughter, Matilda.

"This place is at the back end of nowhere," Suzy Greco said as she barged past him into the hallway. "Trust you to want to live out here."

Greco had no idea why she'd come, but she looked flustered. Suzy was blonde and pretty. She always made the most of herself, always wore makeup and had her hair done, but not tonight. Tonight she looked a mess.

"Whatever you've got cooking smells nice." She smiled faintly. "I hope you've enough left for Matilda." She set down a holdall and a small suitcase on the sofa.

"Go put the holdall in your room, Matilda," she said.

"It's not my turn until the weekend," he said, puzzled.

"You're her father, Stephen. You have to be prepared to shoulder some of the responsibility even when it's not your turn. There are times when I can't do this on my own."

Something was wrong; ordinarily Suzy would never say such a thing. She looked tired, stressed.

"You're not on your own, that's why I moved up here. I want to help, you know that."

"Well, now's your chance."

He noticed her tear-stained face.

"Whatever's wrong, Suzy? Are you okay?"

"No, I'm not. It's been a pig of a day at work, and to top it all, my father's had a heart attack," she said, dissolving into tears.

"Oh, I see." He was struggling. What did she expect from him? Should he comfort her, sit her down and talk it through? But he didn't, he couldn't. He simply stood watching her, not daring to reach out in case she got the wrong idea and bit his head off. Besides which, despite the bad news the only thing he could think about was his job, selfish as that was. This was going to change things. Suzy's parents lived miles away in Norfolk. She was an only child, her parents' sole support. She'd need to be with them, take care of her mother, and her father, Ron, once he was getting better. "So what are you going to do?"

"What do you think, Stephen? I'm going to Cromer. I'm leaving now. I've got compassionate leave from work and I'm not sure when I'll be back."

"And Matilda?"

"I can hardly take her, can I?" she said, exasperated that he'd had to ask. "You know how she idolises him. She can't see her grandad so ill; it'll upset her too much. He might not make it," she added softly, hanging her head. "So you don't have a choice; you must look after her," she told him firmly.

"For how long?" He was floundering on all sorts of fronts now. No other human beings had the ability to affect him like these two. Matilda he loved unreservedly — and Suzy? The truth was he wasn't sure. The divorce had upset him and he hadn't seen it coming — other people had. In fact most folk were surprised they'd lasted as long as they had.

He had work, and he was busy. He glanced at the files on his desk. He couldn't take Matilda to the station so what would he do with her? He looked at Suzy. She meant this; she had that look on her face.

"Like I said, Stephen, you are her father. Step up to the bloody plate and stop pissing about," she said wiping her eyes. "Look I'm sorry — I shouldn't speak to you like that. I know you don't like it but I'm at the end of my tether."

"What about my work?"

"What the hell do you think I do every day?"

She was staring at him with her hands on her hips. Greco didn't like the anger in her eyes.

"Matilda goes to school, then the club they run afterwards and I pick her up at five. I've written it all down for you." She handed him a sheet of paper. "Her school uniform is in the case."

"Five," he said weakly. "Sometimes I can't leave that early." The truth was he never left that early, but she didn't look in the mood to listen to this.

"Well, for the foreseeable you will do — have you got that, Stephen? Matilda needs stability. She's had enough upset with the divorce and the move."

"And whose fault was that?" The words were out before he could stop them.

"Go on, Stephen. Tell me how stupid I've been dragging us all up here to a town we don't know. Tell me I've been a selfish cow and how my actions have ruined your career."

He was in no mood for a row; anyway, this wasn't a battle he could win. He might think all those things but he'd never said them, and he'd been tempted to. "Okay — we'll be fine," he finally conceded. What was the use? "You go, give your mother my love, and I hope your dad pulls through."

She nodded and her expression lightened, that was obviously what she wanted to hear. Ranting at him had probably helped too; it always had in the past.

"Are you going tonight?"

She nodded again.

"You're in a state, are you sure that's wise? It's a long drive."

"Wise or not, Stephen, I'm going. I'll text you when I get there and I'll ring Matilda tomorrow."

He watched her disappear into Matilda's bedroom — to say her goodbyes no doubt.

"She's fine; she won't give you any trouble."

At that his ex-wife left.

Chapter 9

Tuesday

Greco was rifling through his wardrobe. The weather up here was colder than in Norfolk. Granted there had often been a chilly east wind but not the cold, damp air that seemed to be the norm up here. He took out his dark grey suit, a shirt and a woollen overcoat. That should keep him warm enough.

"Am I going to school?" Matilda asked her dad.

"Yes, Tillyflop, and I'm going to take you. Do you want a packed lunch?" Despite not liking nicknames, he had always used this term of endearment for his daughter.

"No, I have dinners. Can I have my hair in plaits?"

She was standing in his kitchen in her nightie with her long blonde hair wafting around her face. He'd have to do something with it, but plaits!

"You've had your shower; why don't you get dressed and I'll do your egg. Toastie soldiers?"

She nodded and marched off back to her bedroom.

It was slow-going. Matilda was easily distracted. She wanted the telly on, then she'd start to play with the stuff she'd brought. At this rate he'd be horribly late.

"We have to go soon," was all he seemed to say to her. "Get ready, there's a good girl."

Finally they were in the car. It was early, not quite eight so he couldn't drop her at school yet. He had no choice; he'd have to take her to the station for a short while. He'd managed to read through the three files the previous night, once he'd got Matilda to bed. Rose Donnelly was a missing-person case and she might yet turn up given she had money to spend. The tobacco scam had been on-going for so long that he couldn't see a little longer making much difference, regardless of what the DCI said.

But the Brenda Hirst file had been interesting. He needed to speak to Julian Batho about the forensics. He had some interesting theories about what was used to remove her eyes and who Brenda had spoken to before she met her end.

The team were all at their desks when he arrived. He was so intent on getting Matilda settled with something to amuse her that he didn't notice the looks they exchanged.

"This is Matilda, my daughter," Greco announced to them. "I'll take her to school shortly so she won't be here long."

"The DCI has been looking for you, sir," George told him.

"Sit here and be a good girl," he told his daughter, giving her a pack of crayons he'd brought from home and a sheet of paper. "I won't be long."

* * *

When he'd gone Grace Harper left her desk and went to talk to the girl. "That's a nice uniform." She smiled. "It's the Duke Academy, isn't it?"

Grace knew this was a private school in Leesworth. She also knew that it must be costing the DI a bomb to send his daughter there.

Matilda didn't answer. Instead she said, "My mummy has had to go away and my daddy can't do plaits."

"He's had a go though, hasn't he?" Grace said, smiling. "But daddies aren't very good at things like that. Would you like me to fix them for you?"

Matilda nodded. "He couldn't find my ribbons either."

"I might have some nice bobbles. I'll get my brush and we'll have you sorted in no time."

By the time Grace had finished Matilda had a splendid pair of plaits finished off with a pair of colourful bobbles from the DC's drawer.

"You look lovely now. You'll have all the boys after you."

Matilda laughed at that.

"Are you staying with your daddy for long?" George asked, joining the conversation.

"I think so. My grandad's ill so Mummy has to look after him and granny for a while. I'm sleeping in my princess bed at Daddy's place."

"I have a little girl," Grace told her, "she's called Holly and she's about your age — five is it?"

Matilda nodded. "But I'm nearly six."

"Why don't you draw daddy a picture to stick on the wall there," Grace suggested, pointing to the empty space above his desk.

"He's not going to find this easy going, is he?" George said.

"No, but by the time he's finished he might have a little more sympathy for my plight," Grace responded. "But it can't harm, can it, the DI having to roll up his sleeves and get on with the childcare on a full-time basis for a while."

* * *

"There's been a tip-off of sorts, Stephen." DCI Green greeted him with the words as he entered his office. The man was looking tired again. "I've had DI Walkden from the serious crime squad on. "Apparently there's a terrorist cell in Oldston." He threw his hands in the air. "I don't know how they came up with that one, but it's all we need. All the stuff we've got going on already plus a load of bomb-happy hooligans on the loose."

"Do they know that for sure, sir? Is the information genuine?"

"Call me Colin," he reminded him. "The counterterrorism unit reckon they've intercepted some messages sent via the dark web to known people in Syria. Those messages started life here in Oldston."

"Do they know what's planned? Was the threat specific?"

"No, but of course we have to be vigilant. Keep our eyes and ears open on the street. Someone might let something slip but I doubt it. This lot are tight. I'm surprised we know as much as we do."

"How involved are we expected to get — given that the unit is on the case?"

"We wait and see. If they want anything, then they'll say, but it'll be at a moment's notice so we have to be ready. But no heroics, we're just small cogs in a much bigger machine."

"The team are up to their eyes, sir — Colin. The murder, the tobacco scam and the possibility of a missing woman . . . I don't have any spare hands."

"I know that. For now brief your team on the merits of staying vigilant, but we don't want rumours spreading. They must not let this leave the station. You get my drift?"

Greco nodded. "Is that all?"

"For now. If anything else occurs then I'll keep you posted."

Terrorists — how likely was that? Greco wondered as he walked the corridor back to the main office. Fair enough, Oldston had a large Asian population but that meant nothing. Plus, there hadn't been any past incidents involving Oldston.

"Daddy look, Grace did my hair!" Matilda spun around. She was pleased as punch.

"You look lovely," he said, picking her up and kissing her forehead. "But it's time for school now." He looked at Grace. "Thanks. I'm hopeless at that sort of thing."

She smiled and winked at Matilda.

"I'll take her to school now. It should take me about half an hour to go there and get to the Duggan Centre. Sergeant, meet me there — half an hour, no later. We'll have a word with Professor Batho —see what he's got for us. Grace, would you work with Craig on the mobile phone numbers?"

"The phone has gone to the Duggan, sir."

"Yes, but we still have a file of the numbers called and rung, don't we? If Brenda did speak to someone minutes before her death, then we need to know who that was. You could try ringing a few, see if we can get anything that helps."

* * *

Once the DI had left, Quickenden flopped forward on his desk, his head in his hands. He hadn't slept all night. He'd been too wound up. He'd been a first class idiot. He'd gambled away all that money but what was worse he'd lost to Geegee and he hadn't a cat in hell's chance of paying off his debt.

"Why the fuck didn't you stop me?" he fired at Craig Merrick. "You just sat there and let me carry on. Now I'm in one helluva mess."

Craig was poring over a computer screen with Grace. "I tried but you were having none of it. You've only got yourself to blame."

"That's no bloody help. I've gone and got myself in hock to Geegee — you do know what that means? He'll rack up the interest and I'll never be free of him. If I pay late, even once, he'll knock my flaming head off."

"You're a cop, he wouldn't dare," Merrick assured him.

"That's not how Geegee sees me though, is it? He sees the old me, the reprobate that used to hang around the estate and cause bother, the one he's had to cuff around the ear on several occasions for giving him cheek."

"He did it on purpose," Merrick told him, turning round to face him, "and I did try to warn you but you weren't having any. He baited you by letting you win. Just enough to whet your appetite and then he took you for all he could. And those cards were marked."

With that he turned back to look at the computer screen with Grace.

"The bastard — I'll bloody swing for him!" Quickenden protested as the penny dropped. "Wait till I find him, I'll make him wish he'd never been born!"

"Calm down, Speedy," Grace advised. "Realistically, what can you do? You'll lose more than a few bob if you go around making threats like that."

Good advice, but Quickenden was in no mood to listen. "Job or no job, when I've finished he'll think twice before messing with my head again."

He was furious. He got up from his desk and started to pace across the office floor. "How d'you know anyway? I didn't see any marks." He was confused. Here was Merrick telling him he'd been conned and he hadn't seen it, not even suspected.

"My dad played cards. He was an expert and he showed me how it's done." He shook his head. "You were had, mate, and there's nowt you can do about it. Take it as a lesson learned and don't get roped in again."

"A bloody expensive lesson." Quickenden had had enough. He turned on his heel without another word and left the office. He'd had enough. He'd have to find some way to teach that crazy bastard a lesson. But how did you get the better of Grady Gibbs?

Chapter 10

Greco couldn't see Quickenden's car in the Duggan Centre car park when he arrived. He sat for a few minutes and waited before ringing the station.

"Grace, where's Quickenden? Has he left?"

There was too long a pause for Greco's liking. Grace was obviously wondering what to tell him. Something was going on.

"He's not there, is he?" he said, letting her off the hook at last. "And it's my guess that you don't know where he's gone."

"Look, sir, we're all busy. He left, he was angry about something. I'm sure he'll turn up."

But Greco was sure of no such thing. The man was about to use up the last of his nine lives. "In that case why don't you meet me here? I'll get a coffee and wait for you in the centre café."

If Quickenden didn't want the opportunity to prove his skills, then he wouldn't waste any more of his time. He'd see how DC Harper got on instead. Her lateness was one thing but there was nothing wrong with her attitude towards the job, and that was what counted.

* * *

"He wants me there instead of Speedy," she told the others triumphantly, once she'd put the phone down. "He's gone and done it now. I'd no idea what to say. I daren't lie, the DI would have known. I mean where the hell is Speedy? He wouldn't really go after Geegee, would he?"

She watched Craig Merrick give an indifferent shrug, and shook her head in response. "He's a bloody idiot. He'll get it this time and I did warn him. Greco isn't like Leighton, he won't stand for it."

"Why you? Why not ask me to go and join him?" Merrick asked.

"Because you probably can't do plaits either," she giggled. "I knew it would pay dividends. He needs nurturing, our new DI, then he'll come round. He's got to be human or he wouldn't have such a lovely little girl."

"Keep it real," Merrick warned her.

"And you keep your comments to yourself."

Grace suspected that the real reason was that Greco had recognised that she had the right attitude to the job. Speedy had pushed it once too often. Merrick was okay but he was a plodder and too fond of clinging to Speedy's coat-tails. If she got this right, then he might include her in the exciting stuff more often. Research was all very well, but Grace enjoyed being out there, gathering the detail and learning from someone who really knew the job.

"While we're out, try and get hold of Speedy on his mobile. Tell the idiot to get his arse back here quick, and to have his excuse polished."

* * *

"Professor Batho?" Greco asked the receptionist.

"Along the corridor — lab number two, on the right-hand side."

"Have you met Batho before?" he asked Grace as they walked.

"No, but he knows a friend of mine, a DC who works at Leesdon."

"Have you spent time with him?"

"Yes, but only the once."

Julian Batho nodded at DI Greco as he walked through the door of his lab.

"Hello again, Inspector, and . . ."

"DC Harper, one of my team," Greco replied, introducing Grace.

"I'm glad you came. I've a number of results for you and I'm sure they'll prove useful."

Greco had worked with the newly appointed professor only once before and it hadn't been a happy experience. The case had ended well but Greco had been sidelined by the team at Leesdon — a team led by DI Calladine, a friend of Batho's.

But on the plus side, the professor had now moved away from Leesdon. His new job was to provide a service to any force that was prepared to pay for it. He had no particular loyalties anymore.

Batho was tall; some would say gangly, he had abnormally long arms and legs. His facial features were large, particularly his nose, but he must have something that appealed to the opposite sex because Greco knew he was seeing a particularly attractive DC at Leesdon. One thing the DI was sure of was that Batho was good at his job. He didn't waste words, took his work very seriously and didn't suffer fools. Theoretically, they had a lot in common.

"The blood in the boot of the sports car was bovine," he began. "Might I suggest from a joint of beef?" he said with a rare smile.

That could make sense. Brenda Hirst had been shopping.

"More significantly, she had traces of an oily substance under her fingernails. Dirty oil, the type you'd find in a garage. If you come up with anything that you think might match, let me have it."

He picked up the folder with the report in it and read through for a few seconds. "There was nothing remarkable about the stomach contents. She hadn't been drinking and there were no drugs evident in her system. She was pregnant as you know and I'm still working on the foetal DNA. I'm also still working on what might have been used to take her eyes out."

Greco was still thinking about the oil thing. Had Brenda possibly tried to defend herself against someone wearing overalls?

"Were there any fabric fibres with the oil?"

"No, and given the oil we did look.

"You've looked at the car, what about the phone? She received a call from someone just minutes before she died. I've had my team trying to find out who from but so far they've got nothing."

"We've looked at that too, Inspector. She was called using a phone belonging to one Rose Donnelly."

"How did you discover that so easily?"

"Because we have a department here that exists solely to find out such things," he informed them. "In future you'd do well to hand such jobs over to us straight away and not waste time."

Greco knew what Green would say to that. It'd do the budget no good at all. Still, this time it had paid dividends.

"Rose Donnelly is missing. I wasn't aware that she knew Brenda but she must have done."

"Or her phone was stolen," Batho suggested, handing Greco the folder.

"How's Imogen?" Grace asked, once the conversation about the forensics had come to an end. "I haven't seen her in a while — work, the kid, you know how it is. We were at police college together. We had some fun back then, believe me."

Julian Batho turned and regarded the young DC. "Imogen is fine. Ring her; I'm sure she'd love to catch up."

* * *

"Back to the nick, sir?"

"Yes — we need to bring the team up to speed with what we've just learned, particularly about the Rose Donnelly connection."

"What time do you collect your daughter?" Grace asked as they drove back.

"Five. Hopefully it'll work out. If not then I'll have to rethink."

"It's tricky — been there and got the T-shirt," she said. "People don't realise the problems one-parent families have. Your wife manages though, doesn't she, sir?"

"Ex-wife, and she works regular hours, so her situation is different."

"During the school holidays I sometimes send Holly to a kid's club in town. They can stay until seven in the evening, if needs be , and they get their meals."

Greco didn't fancy that. Matilda was just getting used to the kids at the Duke Academy. Thrusting her into the varied mix that was Oldston wasn't what he wanted.

"She's a lucky girl going to the Duke. It costs a fortune and the uniform and all the stuff they need isn't cheap either," Grace continued.

"My ex-wife's parents pay Matilda's fees. It's very good of them. Neither Suzy or I want her going to an overcrowded primary school where discipline is an issue."

"The primary near me got 'outstanding' at the last Ofsted. She'll have to mix with Oldston folk sooner or later."

"Yes, but not yet. She isn't ready. She's completely guileless and would be an easy target for a bully."

Grace pulled a face. "I understand that, more than most," she rolled her eyes. "But Oldston's not that bad, not really."

"I still don't think she's ready."

"You can't protect her forever. Kids have to mix and learn how to cope with all kinds. I had to, I had no choice," she admitted. "I had no well-heeled family to pay fees for me."

"So even you had problems as a child?" He was surprised. She appeared to him to be the type who had always been able to fight her corner.

"As a kid, I was overweight," she said. "I was picked on, called names, and I hated it. But I did fight back. Being big can have advantages," she laughed. "Not that I enjoyed it. As I grew up I thinned out and ended up as you see me now."

Greco admired her attitude. He'd not been so brave. The truth was he'd been bullied all through school — and that had been in rural East Anglia. He hadn't fought back, he'd simply gritted his teeth and tried to ignore it. It had been his odd habits, counting or avoiding cracks in the pavement, that had drawn attention to him. What the residents of Oldston might do to a sensitive child like Matilda terrified him. The Duke Academy was where she'd stay for now.

* * *

"A uniformed PC visited the Roberts family, sir. Apparently the problem was solved by Mr Percival Webb himself within a week of the argument," Merrick said, reading from his notes.

"Okay — so they'd no reason to take it further. Did you get a statement from him, Constable?"

Merrick nodded and lifted a sheet from the desk in front of him. "Also Brenda stopped going to the knitting club weeks ago," he added. "Perhaps she used it as an excuse to see Reader?"

"But Reader insisted the relationship was over," Greco reiterated.

"He could have been lying."

"We will have to check that but for now we have a much more important lead." Greco told the team what he'd learned from Julian Batho — all except Quickenden, that was, who was still missing. Greco didn't ask about him.

"When we see Rose, or when we search her place, we'll need to look for any evidence that the two women knew each other. Because if they didn't then we need to know who used Rose's phone to make that final call to Brenda."

"Rose could have lost it, sir," Merrick suggested.

"Bit of a coincidence though, isn't it?" George added. "We now have an address for her. She lives on the Link estate."

"We need to go round there. If she isn't at home then we must get access."

"What happened to the shopping Brenda had with her when she got into Reader's car, sir? The blood tells us it went in the boot but it's not there now and it wasn't littering the canal bank when we found her," Grace spoke up.

"The killer could have taken it." Merrick shrugged. "Her personal possessions were taken so why not her shopping too?"

"Do we have any more information about those possessions?" Greco looked at his team. No one was volunteering anything. "Craig, go and talk to Jack Hirst. Find out about her handbag, any money she was carrying, bank cards, that sort of thing. Also, something was ripped from her wrist. What was it, a watch or bracelet? Get a description."

Greco continued, "With regards to the oil, there are a number of firms on the industrial estate down there, so we'll start with them. I want to know who wears overalls and gets them oily. Take samples where you can and Professor Batho will analyse them."

"Reader has a garage as well as the showroom, sir," George told them while continuing to tap away on her computer keyboard. "It's on that industrial estate."

"Another reason to speak to Mr Reader again."

"He's at home, sir."

"Then that's where we'll go next." He nodded at Grace. "We're dealing with a vicious killer so I don't want anyone going off on their own. We appear to be one man down." He sighed at Quickenden's absence. "Grace and I will see Reader, and then we'll go to the address we've got for Rose. Craig you take a PC and visit Jack Hirst and then on to the industrial estate and see what you can get. Ask if anyone saw anything on Saturday. Take those samples and pay particular attention to what the staff at Reader's garage have to say. Note everything down."

The office phone rang.

"Professor Batho, sir," said George, handing it to Greco.

"It's almost certain that the implement used to remove Brenda Hirst's eyes was a potato peeler," he told the detective.

"On what evidence do you base that theory?"

"There was a tiny residual trace of potato fluid on the skin around the eye sockets," he explained. "Also the shape of the wound would fit."

"Was this done post-mortem?"

"Thankfully, yes, Inspector — no blood."

Greco put the phone back and was silent for a few seconds.

"Our killer used a potato peeler to gouge out Brenda's eyes," he told the team. He saw Grace wince. "He needs catching before some other poor soul falls into his grasp."

Chapter 11

"Have you found the bastard yet?"

Greco regarded the woman. She looked angry. Her hair was wild, untended, and despite it being lunchtime she was still wearing a dressing gown.

"After you lot took him yesterday he came back, grabbed a few things and scarpered. Whatever you said got him rattled. He was a bag of nerves before he left."

Greco could think of nothing they'd said that could have made him run. Reader had been quite candid about Brenda and the pregnancy, so what was going on? "Mrs Reader, Do you know where he could have gone?" The man was a damn nuisance. Now they'd have to waste time and resources trying to find him.

"No idea — unless he's shacked up with one of his tarts." She rubbed her face. "That wouldn't surprise me. That's what this is all about, isn't it? Something's happened and he's in it right up to his neck."

"Does he have a relative or a friend he could have gone to?"

"The bastard's having another affair, isn't he? I'm not daft — he's gone to some woman. He hasn't even rung me

— just left, and never said a word about when he'd be back. He doesn't even try to hide it anymore."

"How do you know he's seeing someone else?" Greco asked.

"Because the idiot's a chronic womaniser, and I recognise the signs; that's how I know. They're usually blonde and stupid, but occasionally he does go off track." She ran a hand through her unkempt hair. "So come on — who's the sad bitch this time?"

"We can't say," answered Greco. "We're here to speak to your husband. The matter he's been helping us with is the murder of a woman in Oldston."

At this she looked genuinely shocked and shook her head. "He'd never harm anyone, not Alex. He's good with the chat-up lines and he can't keep his hands to himself, but apart from that he's harmless."

"Did he take his car?"

"Yes, that bloody sports job he's so fond of. Look . . ." She paused for a moment. "He's taken his passport," she admitted. "He won't fly so he'll be heading for a port somewhere."

"Thank you, Mrs Reader. You've been a great help."

Greco and Grace got back in their car. "Grace, ring the station and get Georgina to alert the ports, and the airports too. He might not like flying but he's acting desperate. Get her to circulate Alex Reader's photo. We need to speak to him. I want to know why he ran."

Greco drove them back along the ring road into Oldston and then onto the Link estate. A road known as Link Road ran all the way round its circumference, and it was busy. People used it as a shortcut to the ring road and then onto the motorway network.

"Where does Rose Donnelly live?"

"The bottom flat in a block of five. It's that one, sir," she pointed. "Alderley House."

It had started to rain; the building was constructed out of grey concrete blocks, which made it look even more drab and uninviting. The bottom flat had two plant pots on either side of the door, but the small conifers in them had died off months ago. A woman was banging on the door and shouting through the letterbox.

"Damn cheek," she said, as Greco approached. "Two grand she's given me, well, I don't want her money. Blood money that's what it is. Stupid cow thinks she can ease her conscience by bribing me with this." She waved an envelope at them. "Well, she's wrong. Nothing could put right what she did."

Neither of the detectives had any idea what she was talking about.

"Do you know where Rose Donnelly is?" Greco asked.

"No. Gone off to spend some of that money of hers." She sniffed and pushed the envelope through the letterbox. "There! She can keep her bribe. I want none of it."

"Can I ask what all this is about?" Grace asked. "What did she give you the money for?"

The woman looked warily from him to Grace.

"It's nothing, an old matter, goes back years. It's something that's sorted now, no sense bringing it up again." She sniffed again. "Anyway, I don't want her money. I'd do it again."

"She paid you money to keep quiet about something?" Grace asked.

"Yes, well, no, not really, she felt guilty about the way she'd lived back then, the things she'd done and the people she'd hurt. I lived around here then so I know things. Now that she's come up in the world she wants me to keep quiet. It's a pay-off really"

"And she hurt you?"

Greco watched her wrestle with the reply, her face a picture of indecision.

"Yes, I suppose she did in a way, but it worked out okay, so no harm done."

As far as Greco was concerned, this was wasting time. This woman could rattle on for hours and they'd still be none the wiser. "Would anyone around here have a key to the flat?" He asked patiently.

"Her two doors up, she'll have one."

"Can I ask your name?" Grace asked, "just in case we need to speak again."

"Mavis Bailey. I live four streets that way, ask anyone."

"Intriguing, sir." Grace remarked. "Wonder what happened for Rose to give the woman two thousand quid?"

"None of our business, Constable. If it's nothing to do with the case then we don't want to know."

Greco could tell from her face that that wasn't how Grace saw things. She was curious and that was good but for now they needed to get on with the task in hand.

The inside of Rose's flat gave very little away. But it didn't look as if she'd gone anywhere. The place was untidy. There were pots stacked up in the sink and the cat was asleep on the sofa. As they entered it rushed to them, mewing.

"I think it's hungry," Grace decided. "I'll give it something and have a word with the neighbour."

"If Rose hasn't left the cat in her care then you're right, she probably hasn't gone away. So where is she?"

Greco's mobile was ringing. He went outside to take the call. When he rejoined Grace he didn't look too happy. "I'm going to have to leave," he told her.

"Just let me take this back and see what the neighbour says." Grace waved the key at him.

When Grace returned to the car Greco was tapping impatiently on the steering wheel.

"Well, Rose hasn't gone away. She always leaves instructions for the cat with her neighbour and she knows nothing."

"We need to find her. I only hope she's not in the same situation Brenda found herself in."

"Where to now, sir?"

"I'll drop you at the station but I'm going to have to go and pick Matilda up I'm afraid. Apparently the heating's gone in the school. I tell you, there's always something."

"Fixing it could take time. What have they said?"

"Nothing that helps; just that they'll be shut for a few days."

That gave him one huge problem. What was he going to do with a small child while he worked? There was no one else, and he wasn't expecting Suzy back any time soon.

"There is the kids' club, sir. It takes all ages and for any number of reasons. You need somewhere, someone," she insisted. "I'll give you the number." She jotted it down on a piece of paper and left it on the dashboard.

She had that no nonsense look on her face. The one Greco was fast coming to recognise. Grace Harper had it in her to be bossy, confrontational. The way her life had made her, he supposed. It seemed a shame to him that she didn't have someone to share her problems with. She wasn't unattractive. He knew she was only twenty-six, but she looked older than that.

"I'm not sure . . ." He looked at the number and shook his head. There could be all sorts at a place like that. Matilda has led such a sheltered life. I'm afraid Suzy and her parents have seen to that."

"The kids do seem to like it though, sir. I know Holly does. Sometimes she goes there and sometimes my mum takes her. Would you like me to ask my mum if she'd have Matilda? She is a registered child minder. I'm sure she wouldn't mind."

"Where does she live, your mum?"

"Not far from Oldston Park. She's inspected regularly and everything. She's very nice."

It was a very kind offer, but should he accept it? "I'll think about it."

"If you like, your Matilda can come round to mine later, have her tea with Holly and meet my mum. The girls are the same age and if she had a friend, then Matilda wouldn't feel so strange."

It was nice of Grace to do this. She was going out of her way to be helpful. Was it that she sympathised, or was there something else? He wasn't stupid; she was a young woman with no man in her life. He'd have to be careful. He didn't want to encourage a romance where one wasn't going to happen.

Greco nodded, and thanked Grace. Despite his reservations, it was certainly worth thinking about.

* * *

Speedy was at the Spinners. "You seen Geegee?" he asked.

"He was kicking about outside a while ago, bothering a couple of teenagers," he replied. "Gave one a bit of a kicking and dragged him off. He'll be back, he'll need a pint after all that exertion." He laughed.

So Geegee was in bash 'em and stuff the consequences mode. Speedy cursed and took a swig of the beer Les handed him.

"Took a packet off you last night." The landlord pulled a face. "Must have hurt, even for someone like you with a regular job."

"Did sting a bit," Speedy said. "What d'you think the chances are of him doing a deal?"

"Not a cat in hell's chance, mate," laughed Les. "He'll have you strung up first."

Jed Quickenden couldn't remember a time when he'd been in so much trouble. He'd ballsed things up at work but worse than that, much worse, he was about to tell Geegee he couldn't pay his debt. The man might kill him. It most certainly wouldn't be pretty. He slammed the empty pint pot on the counter and shouted for Les. "Stick another one in there and give us a whiskey too."

He looked around; there was only one or two in. "D'you do much lunchtime trade?"

"Not really, don't do food you see, but I don't mind if folk bring their own." He nodded at a young man seated in a corner munching his sandwiches.

"Who is that? I've seen him in here at night once or twice recently."

"I've no idea. He's hatching some plot with Geegee. Probably doesn't know what he's getting into, poor sucker."

Speedy downed the whiskey, grabbed his pint and went to sit down beside the lad. "Don't mind, do you?" he smiled. "I'm looking for Geegee. Are you meeting him here?"

"You're that cop, aren't you?"

Quickenden nodded. "Not a problem is it? Geegee never bothered about my day job."

"Perhaps, but I'm a bit pickier." The lad smirked. "I don't like coppers; too nosey."

"Only doing a job, son," he said, taking a gulp of his beer. "Currently we're investigating the murder of a woman. She was found just along the canal from here."

"Nowt to do with me."

"I'm not saying it is. We're speaking to lots of people." He looked into the boy's face, he was good-looking with fair hair and smallish features, but he had strange eyes. For a few seconds, Quickenden was almost mesmerised. They were the coldest eyes he'd ever seen.

"How well do you know Geegee?" Quickenden asked.

He watched the boy frown. "Well enough," he said putting a half- eaten sandwich back into his plastic box. "You?"

"I've known Geegee since I was a schoolboy. He was always the big man around here. Everyone was scared of him but he was a useful bloke to know."

The boy nodded.

"You're dressed for work," the sergeant said, glancing at his overalls. "Not many people Geegee knows actually hold down a job. What are you up to?"

"Nowt. I come here because I like it," he admitted. "It's edgy, the people are hard, raw, I get a buzz from that. Me and some of my friends come quite often. You can buy anything you want, if you know what I mean." He smiled.

Was he talking drugs? The no-hopers who came here would see him as an outsider, a kid after kicks, and they'd be only too happy to accommodate him. Speedy was surprised no one had tried it on, taken advantage. "Don't you get picked on when you come in here? I mean with you being different?"

"I'm no different from them, not really. I work because I have to. Anyway you've got no right to talk, copper, look what you do for a living."

He was about to buy the lad another pint when Geegee walked in.

Speedy felt his stomach lurch. If he got out of here without a beating, he'd be lucky. "I need a word with him," he told the boy, pulling a face.

"You owe him, don't you?" the boy whispered. "I heard you lost at cards. He's a hard man with a brute of a temper. Not very wise of you, that."

"Unfortunately, yes, I did and now I'm going to suffer for it."

"Do you like him?"

"God no — I hate the slimy bastard, he's evil. I really should avoid him, and so should you. Take my advice; leave this pub well alone before you get into serious trouble. It's a cesspit, no place for a lad like you."

"He sells some great stuff though," the boy nodded, "as long as you don't ask too many questions. He had a watch the other night, a solid gold job it was, and he only wanted fifty quid for it. I was hoping to get it for my mum's birthday but he ended up giving it to that woman, that Lily, who hangs out here."

"Did you ask him about it?"

"Yes, but it wasn't suitable," he shrugged. "It had initials engraved on the back, *AH*. My mum's *VP*, so you see the problem."

"Copper!" Geegee interrupted from the bar. "Come to pay your debts?" He chuckled.

"I'd better go and pacify him," Speedy said leaving the lad to his lunch.

"We need to talk." He approached with caution. "You took a packet off me last night and now I know you cheated."

"Me? Come on, copper, does that sound right? When have you ever known me to be dishonest?" He laughed out loud. His breath stank and he was still wearing the clothes he'd had on during the game. "Pay up, copper," he taunted. "Because you know what happens if you don't."

"Can we speak outside?"

"Shy about folk seeing you give me all that money?" He laughed again as he followed Speedy outside.

"Look, Geegee, I'm not going to wrap this up. I can't pay."

There. It was said. There was a silence. What was the bastard thinking? "It's impossible; I just don't have that much money right now. But I'll sort something out. I'll get a loan, but you've got to give me more time."

The DS inhaled, and readied himself. This wasn't going to be good. But he was wrong. Instead of landing one on his chin, Grady Gibbs put his arm around Speedy and led him away from the pub door. Being so close turned Speedy's stomach.

"Just this once I'm going to let it go," Geegee said.

Speedy stood stock still and stared at the man. This wasn't right. Geegee didn't operate like this.

"Why? I don't understand."

"Well, let's put it this way," he said, giving him an almost toothless smile. "Giving you time to find the dosh could pay dividends. It's a good move on my part — a favour in the bank. A favour I might need to call in very soon." He winked at the sergeant. "Relax." He clapped Speedy on the back. "You got off light and don't forget it. You owe me."

* * *

"I haven't got long," he told the team, checking his watch. "What have we got out of this afternoon's investigations?" Greco shuffled pieces of paper around the desk, neatening them into piles. He'd go over them again when things were quieter, make sure he hadn't missed anything. He'd taken Grace, Craig Merrick and George into the small meeting room to talk. He'd have to make it quick. The headmistress at the Duke Academy was looking after Matilda in her office until he picked her up and he'd promised to do so within the hour.

"Jack Hirst has no idea what Brenda kept in her handbag, sir. Her purse, he presumes and she did have a debit card. He can't find it in the house, so it must have been taken. As for cash, he reckons about a tenner, tops. Also he's adamant that neither of them knew Rose Donnelly."

"So it was hardly robbery, then."

"So why was she a target? Why murder her and take her eyes like that?"

"A trophy," Craig commented. "It's common with serial killers, I understand."

"But have we got a serial killer? We have the one body, and that looks more like a revenge killing to me," responded Greco.

"Revenge for what, sir? Apart from her affair with Reader, she appears to have led a fairly simple life," said Grace. "But that said, could we be looking at Reader's wife?"

"Check on Mrs Reader's movements on Saturday, Craig. Get statements, I don't want any 'maybes.' Make sure you pin the evidence down."

"We mustn't forget about Rose Donnelly. No one's seen her recently and her home is like the Marie Celeste," Grace told them.

"So what are we saying?" Greco looked around from one to the other only to be met by blank looks. "Do we think Rose is dead too? If so, why hasn't a body turned up? Brenda was found within hours."

At that moment they heard the main office door open. Quickenden, Greco guessed. The DI got up and told him to come into the meeting room. He wanted to blast the man but now wasn't the time. He'd take the sergeant to task about his behaviour tomorrow.

"I don't know where you've been, Sergeant, but you'll have time to explain yourself, just make it good. Your job depends on it. For now sit down and keep quiet."

"The jewellery around her wrist was a watch, sir," Craig said, consulting his notebook. "It was quite distinctive. It had belonged to Jack Hirst's mother and had her initials on the back. It was left to Brenda after her death. He reckons it was valuable, nine-carat gold. It had originally been a golden wedding anniversary present from Jack's father to his mother."

"Alert the jewellers and pawn shops," he told Craig. "Did he have it insured, or have a photo?"

"No, sir."

"They're unlikely to say anything. If they get their hands on an item like that, they'll have it flogged on in no time," Speedy said.

"Difficult to sell," Merrick contradicted. "With the initials I mean."

What are they?" Speedy asked, knocking Craig's arm.

"I'm sure DC Merrick was coming to that." Greco shot him a warning look. In his book, quiet meant quiet. Merrick had put effort into what he'd done today and had come up with some valuable information. He deserved the opportunity to report back properly.

"It's just that a watch like Craig just described, with the initials *AH* on the back, was given to a woman in the Spinners. She was flashing it about last night."

Greco looked at Quickenden. This was so typical of how things went in the sergeant's life. His job's on the brink of going down the tubes and he pulls this out of the bag. He shook his head. "Are those the right initials?" he asked Craig.

"Yes, sir, they are. The original owner's name, Benda's mother-in-law, was Ada Hirst.

"In that case can we have more detail please, Sergeant?"

"Geegee — real name Grady Gibbs," he explained for Greco's benefit, "gave a watch fitting that description to his latest squeeze very recently. He'd first offered it for sale but because of the initials he couldn't find a buyer. Well, that and the fact that money is short meant no one could afford it."

"In that case we need to speak to this Mr Gibbs. Bring him in," Greco told Quickenden and Merrick. "Stick him in the cells. I'll sort out my daughter and then come back."

Chapter 12

"Sir, if you can do without me, then I'll come with you to pick up Matilda. You could explain things to her then I'll take her to mine for tea with Holly and my mum. It would let you come back here with no pressure."

Greco shut his eyes and inhaled deeply. This wasn't how he wanted to do things. He didn't want to rely on other people, especially colleagues, for anything, but what else could he do? Quickenden and Merrick would bring Grady Gibbs in, but he had to be there at the interrogation.

"Okay," he finally said. "That's very good of you. We'll go now and get things organised."

It was a quick fix for now but even if the Duke Academy hadn't had a problem with the heating, he couldn't guarantee he'd be able to pick his daughter up on time every day. The after school club they ran shut at five. He needed something else and quick. "Your Mum," he inquired as Grace drove them, "would she mind having Matilda? It would mean picking her up from the Duke and it's not central. It'd mean a drive out to Leesworth, but I would pay her," he told Grace.

"I have already mentioned it, sir. She knows it's not for long, so yes she's up for it."

That was something at least. The last thing he needed right now was a childcare issue to worry about. He looked at Grace. Now he understood. She might have her mum handy but it was still a struggle. In future, if she was late, he'd have to bite his tongue. DC Harper had problems the others hadn't a clue about.

* * *

"You okay with this?" Craig Merrick asked Speedy as they drove towards the pub. "I take it you found him this afternoon, Geegee, I mean?"

"Yes I found him and no, I'm not okay with this. I owe him, but what's worse the sneaky bastard wanted to bank my debt as a favour." He slammed his hands on the steering wheel as he drove. "You can imagine what he'll say when I turn up to bring him in."

"Did you threaten him? You were pretty riled up when you left."

"No, not really. I told him I knew he'd cheated, but he doesn't give a stuff. It was him that threatened me. If he wants something and I don't deliver then it'll be me you can look for in the canal," he said grimly. "And I'm not exaggerating either."

It was late afternoon and the Spinners was filling up with the usual faces, including Lily, Geegee's girlfriend.

"That's her," Speedy nodded.

"How do we play this?" He glanced back through the window to the parking space outside. "Backup is in place."

"Good, because we're going to need them. When I arrest Geegee this place will go off like a firecracker. I'll find out where he is and you speak to the girl."

"Excuse me," Merrick said sidling up beside Lily. "DC Merrick, Oldston CID." He flashed his badge. "Mind if I ask you a few questions?"

She laughed in his face and downed her vodka in one. "You sure?" She looked scornful. "I had you down as one of the silly sods who were in the game last night." She giggled. "Never had you down as a copper, too good-looking. Him, yes," she pointed at Speedy. "He's a bloody fool, but you," she stroked a finger down his cheek, "you're cute."

"You were showing us a watch, Lily. Do you have it on today?"

"Beautiful, isn't it?" She showed him. "He's a sentimental bugger underneath all that rough." She grinned at Merrick. "And it's worth a bob or two. When he gets fed up with me, I can cash it in. It's win-win, don't you think?"

"I suppose so." He coughed. "But there is a small problem. I'd like you to come down to the station and give a statement, Lily," Merrick told her. "Just about how you got the watch and how long you've had it."

"I told you, soft lad, Geegee gave it to me." And she pouted. "I don't want to go there, it makes me nervous."

All the time he'd been talking to Lily, Craig had been slowly leading her towards the door. Once he got her there, he pointed to the police car. "These gentlemen will look after you, Lily. No need to worry, they'll won't keep you long and they'll bring you back."

"No way. You can't drag me down there. I'll tell Geegee. He'll sort you, he'll sort the bloody lot of you," she responded angrily. But it was too late.

Speedy stood at the bar, looking around anxiously. He half-expected Geegee to jump him any second. "Where is he?" he asked Les.

The landlord shrugged but his eyes flicked towards the back room.

"Another game going on?"

Les nodded.

He was going to have to bite the bullet. If Geegee got wind of uniform being outside, then he'd scarper. Speedy nodded at Craig and gestured towards the door. "We'll do this together. Give uniform the nod."

He barged straight in. The room was a fog of cigarette smoke and four men were seated around a table.

"Come back for more?" Geegee taunted when he spotted him. "Don't be shy, come in, grab a chair and help yourself from the bottle," he invited, shaking a near-empty whisky bottle at him.

"Come with me, Geegee." Speedy's voice cracked, from the smoke, fear, and the consequences that were sure to follow.

"The lad wants to take me somewhere," Geegee laughed to the others. "There's a cop car outside so they must want me at the nick, what d'you say?"

"Just come with me and we can get this sorted," Speedy tried.

"Get what sorted? The fact that you owe me a packet? How d'you think that'll go down with your bosses, copper?"

"All we want is the answer to a few questions, nothing heavy," Speedy lied. He daren't mention murder or Geegee would be out the window and gone.

"Okay." This surprised everyone. "But you've got to bring me back and this room remains locked while I'm gone," he told the others. "So go on, scarper, the lot of you."

Speedy took that to mean that Geegee was up to his old tricks again; marked cards and a guaranteed winning streak. People like him needed culling.

"What's this about?" he asked Speedy, before he got in the police car.

"My boss wants a word," was all the sergeant would say.

"About you gambling and losing a packet? Or perhaps it's our little deal that's got his interest." He laughed. "You haven't forgotten that, have you, lad? Because I certainly haven't. It's like having cash in the bank." He paused and stared into Speedy's face for a few seconds. "Cash I might have to call on if things get heavy. You will get me out of this if I need you to, won't you, copper?"

"I'm powerless; others much higher up the chain will be running things."

"You're not that stupid. A missing bit of evidence here, a lost statement there; it can be done, so don't go telling me you're powerless," he warned.

Speedy's nerves were unravelling. What would the mad bugger say once he was faced with Greco? He didn't fancy his chances with that one. If the DI got one whiff of that card game and his losses, then Speedy's career would be over.

* * *

When they arrived at the station Craig Merrick explained to Lily that the watch hadn't been Geegee's to give her. She'd argued the point bitterly, but given she could be charged with receiving stolen property, she finally handed it over. By the time Geegee made it to the interview room, the watch was sitting in an evidence bag on the table in front of him.

Geegee sat slumped in a chair, his hands in his pockets. Greco sat opposite and a uniformed officer was at the door.

"Is this the watch you gave to Lily Dawson?" Greco began, tapping the bag. The man was a waster, typical of all that was wrong with the town. Geegee shrugged and shuffled on his chair before leaning forward for a closer look.

"Yeah, looks like it," he said.

"Where did you get it from?"

"Found it, didn't I?" Geegee grinned.

Typical response from a well-seasoned scoundrel who'd been in this position many times before. He'd long since ceased to be intimidated by a police station or a formal interview. He was inviting Greco to disprove what he'd just said. But was he going to do that?

"Where exactly did you find it?"

"By the canal, on the bank before the tall bridge. It was just lying there in the mud."

"Did you find anything else?"

"Why, was there anything else to find?" Geegee coughed and took a filthy handkerchief from his pocket.

"Just answer the question, Mr Gibbs."

"As it happens I did, copper. There was a woman's bag and an empty purse. Someone had been unlucky or dead careless I reckon."

Everything the man was telling him fitted. Brenda Hirst had had a bag with her, containing a purse. "What did you do with them?"

He shrugged again. "No use to me. The purse was empty and I have no use for a handbag. I threw them in the canal."

"When was this? Try and be specific."

"Yesterday morning, not early, I don't do early, so it must have been about eleven thirty. I was walking my dog."

"Was there anyone with you when you found the things?"

"Look, am I under arrest or summat? Only if I'm not, I think I'll be off, things to do." He cleared his throat and slid the chair back from the desk. "You're barking up the wrong tree, copper. I didn't steal that stuff; mugging's not my style, ask anyone."

"Mr Gibbs, we're investigating a murder not a theft. The items you found belonged to the murdered woman." There was a silence. Grady Gibbs's face had paled.

"I ain't killed no one."

"I didn't say you had. I just want to know where you got these items from."

"And if I had killed someone, I wouldn't leave their stuff just lying around. I'm not stupid."

"I'm going to give you a little time to think things over, Mr Gibbs. I want you to consider your position carefully before we resume our talk."

With that, Greco left the interview room.

"Craig, take the watch round to Jack Hirst and make sure it's the right one. Sergeant, what do we know about this character, Grady Gibbs?"

"He's something of an all-rounder, sir. He's into most of the scams that go on in Oldston. He deals drugs, although we've never had enough evidence to build a case. He's not shy about giving anyone who crosses him a good kicking, but to date he's never actually killed anyone. Not to my knowledge, anyway," Speedy added thoughtfully.

"Is he involved in the tobacco smuggling?"

At that Speedy smiled and shook his head. "No, sir, the Hussains won't let him in. They did their best to keep him short on the drugs too. They might be on the wrong side themselves but they've got more sense than to get involved with Geegee."

"He drinks in that pub you go to. Do you know him, would he talk to you?"

"He might, but he's not going to tell me anything that'd drop him in it."

"We'll let him cool his heels for a while then speak to him again. You can sit in this time, Sergeant."

* * *

Greco had gone down to the canteen to get himself some food and Quickenden was beside himself with worry. He'd no idea what Geegee had said or what he was likely to say once Greco went in there again. He had to see him first.

He made a mug of coffee and took it along to the interview room. He nodded at the uniform who let him in and waited outside.

"Here, and it's more than you deserve," he said, slamming the mug on the desk.

117

"I want to know how they found out. I ain't said a word outside the Spinners about that stuff I found, and there isn't anyone in there who'd snitch."

The young lad had let it slip but Quickenden would keep that to himself for the time being.

"You're not going to pin some murder on me, it ain't fair because I didn't do it. If you try, I'll drop you in it so fast you'll wonder what hit. You owe me and you'd do well to keep that in mind."

"Look, Geegee, this isn't down to me. I had nothing to do with your arrest. This is down to the boss and that bloody watch." He watched the man slurp on his drink. "Where did you get the damn thing? Don't give me any bullshit."

"Like I told your boss, I found it on the canal bank. Just lying there in the mud it was."

"And you expect me to believe that?"

"Believe what you like, but this time it's the truth."

"But you can't prove it, can you?"

"No." He thought for a moment. "But you can help me with that."

"I won't be your alibi, there's no way I'll do that. I've gone too far as it is."

"You'll stop whining and do exactly as I tell you."

"I won't lie; the boss will know."

"You've got even less backbone than I thought," Geegee scoffed. "You'll go and see Daz Hopper. You'll tell him what to say. You'll tell him that he was with me yesterday morning and that we walked my dog along the canal. We found the watch, the bag and the purse together. I kept the watch and threw the rest in the canal."

"Will he do it?"

"If he wants to keep his legs, he will."

"Okay, I'll see what I can do."

"You won't see, you'll do it. When your boss gets back I'm going to use Darren as my alibi and then get the hell out of here. You need me to keep quiet about your gambling habit, so don't let me down. Do you understand, copper? "

Speedy understood only too well. He was being forced to do Geegee's dirty work. He had to find some way of sorting this or Geegee would be asking favours forevermore.

Darren Hopper lived on the Link — didn't they all. He was another one who was never out of trouble. Still, if he gave Geegee an alibi, then that got them all out of the mire. But it did mean ducking out again. What to tell the boss?

"George!" She was the only one left in the office. "I feel sick, it's come on suddenly. I've thrown up twice since coming in earlier. I'm going to have to go home." She looked up from her computer and shook her head. "Lifestyle, Speedy, all that drinking and no food. Go home, I'll tell the boss. He'll just have to do without you."

"Lay it on thick will you. Tell him how pale I was and how I was in pain."

She rolled her eyes and nodded. He owed her. Speedy left by the back stairs; he didn't want to bump into Greco coming back. He took his car and made for Link Road. If memory served him right Darren Hopper lived in a flat on the fourth floor of the tower block.

He had to be in, he just had to be, because he didn't have a phone number for him. He banged on the door of one of the flats and it was answered by an elderly woman.

"I'm looking for Darren Hopper." Speedy smiled. "He lives along here somewhere, but I'm not sure where." He flashed his badge.

"Number six and make it stick this time." The woman scowled at him. "He's a right tearaway, drives us all mad with his music and his noise."

Number six. Speedy made his way along the corridor and rapped on the door. Stace answered.

"I'm looking for Darren."

She didn't look pleased; she'd obviously guessed he was a cop.

"Daz, get your arse in here!" she bellowed back along the hallway.

"No, it's alright, I just need a word. He's done nothing wrong," Speedy assured her.

"Leave us, Stace," Daz told her as soon as he appeared.

"I don't have long," Speedy began. "Geegee needs an alibi and you're it."

A few minutes later Darren Hopper was fully versed in what he had to tell Greco when he came calling."

"Wants the bloody lot, he does," Daz complained. "Got me running about all over the place for him but still he's not satisfied."

Speedy didn't have time for curiosity so he let that one go.

"They will ask — you know what to say. Don't get it wrong; remember this is Geegee calling the shots, not me."

Chapter 13

"Anyone know why they're emptying the shopping centre in Manchester?" Quickenden asked.

"No idea, Speedy, where did you hear that?" Craig asked.

"It was on the local radio when I was getting dressed. Shut the place up tight they have and aren't letting anyone in. Something's going on."

"I expect we'll get to know sooner or later."

Grace wasn't listening. She had her diary out and seemed to be working stuff out.

"What are you doing?"

"It's childcare, Speedy," she told him. "The boss has a problem and I'm trying to help."

"Why? I don't get it. What's the man got, to have you running around after him?"

"I like him," she admitted. "He's okay once you get through that barrier he puts up. He's actually quite human, vulnerable even, and he's easy on the eye too." She winked at Speedy.

"You're mad, you. Vulnerable! Are we talking about the same bloke? He's not interested in you, so my advice is don't get involved. He won't stay around here for long, mark my words. He'll get a promotion and be off somewhere else before you've finished batting your eyelashes."

"He came round to mine last night," she boasted. "Stayed for tea and met my mum while his little girl played with Holly."

"Listen to me, don't mix it, girl. You're work colleagues, anything else won't pan out. You're a soft touch and he's using you. It'll end in tears." Quickenden didn't like fraternising with the DIs. He preferred to keep anyone above the rank of sergeant at arm's length.

"What happened to you yesterday, Speedy? You left here in a right state. Get your little problem sorted, did you?" Craig Merrick asked him. "When you didn't come back I was thinking of sending out a search party."

"I went home sick. I left a message for the boss."

"I didn't mean that, I meant with Geegee. You were all set to kill him when you went chasing out of here."

"No need. It worked out fine, no black eyes. Look," he said shaking his head in front of Craig's face. "Weird though, not what I expected," he replied. "And it's no thanks to you either. You could have stopped this. The next time you see some flash bastard dealing dodgy cards, do me a favour and drag me out of the place."

"There was no stopping you though, was there?" Craig reminded him. "Not like Geegee though, to let you off. Is he losing his touch?"

"No, he hasn't, he's just prepared to wait, that's all."

Speedy didn't want to go into any more detail. The fewer people who knew about his little deal, the better.

"That's not like him either, what did you have to threaten him with?"

"Nothing." Speedy shrugged. "It was his idea."

"Whatever you've sorted, you look a lot better today," Grace noted. "Try to stay out of trouble now. I don't think the boss was impressed with your disappearing act and I'm talking both of them!"

"He was a lot less impressed when Geegee came up with that alibi." Merrick pulled a face. "Left it to the death he did, then yanked Darren Hopper out of the bag. The boss let him stew in the cells for the night and left word to let him out this morning."

Quickenden said nothing. He sat at his desk and accessed the local news on his computer. He could only hope that yesterday's actions didn't come back to haunt him. He'd provided a false witness for a known criminal. If it got out then his career was goosed. "Shopping mall is still closed. They're saying it's a bomb threat," he told the others.

Now he had their attention, talk of Grady Gibbs was replaced by something much more interesting. "Apparently there was an anonymous message sent to the papers this morning."

"It'll be a hoax. Kids chancing their arm," Merrick said.

"Stupid thing to do in the current climate," Grace replied.

"Don't think it's a hoax; they've blocked off some of the M62 now. Looks like the real deal to me."

* * *

Greco arrived later than usual, but no one noticed apart from Grace.

"Got Matilda sorted with my mum, sir?" she asked, giving him a big smile.

"Yes. Thanks for that. She likes your Holly, kept on about her all last night." He smiled back at her.

"Have you caught the news, sir?" George asked. "Bomb scare I think."

He looked at the computer screen she was watching. "Turn the sound up, please."

It looked as if DCI Green's information had some truth in it. A grim thought, and he still hadn't briefed the team either.

"We should keep an eye on that. Right, get a cup of coffee, then the meeting room in ten minutes."

He knew what they'd be thinking. More meetings, and what had they got? A big fat nothing. Currently every lead led to a dead end and they were no closer than they'd been on Monday morning.

Greco left them to it and walked along the corridor to the DCI's office.

"You've seen it, then."

"Being so local, serious crime is going with the Oldston call. I've only been told very recently but messages have been floating around the dark net for weeks. Damn near impossible to trace but the clever people in computer forensics say they definitely originated around here."

"How did word about the shopping mall get out?"

"We were given a warning, simple as that."

"That's not how it's worked in recent times, sir. How did we get this warning?"

Three years ago, Greco had been seconded to the Met for a short while. He'd worked with a team set up to disrupt terrorist plots. It had been a hard slog because there was never anything concrete. Mostly it was about keeping an eye on the Muslim youth and who was talking to them. But never once in that time had they received any warnings and that wasn't because there were no plots. It was just that the public were not always made aware of them.

"An email sent to Manchester Central."

"I know we can't take the risk, but it sounds like a hoax."

"You're right, we can't take the risk. If you haven't done so already, then brief your team. At least one of them finds his way into some dodgy corners of this town."

Greco didn't reply; he knew the DCI meant Quickenden. He'd speak to the sergeant himself at the first opportunity.

"I want progress, Stephen," he said with a deep sigh as he changed the subject. "This murder business is going nowhere, according to the report you emailed me this morning."

Greco saw the confusion on the DCI's face.

"Do you never sleep, Stephen? It isn't that I don't appreciate being kept up to date with every step of your investigations but it isn't necessary, particularly when you're still stuck on square one."

"It's how I've always worked, sir."

* * *

"What you doing in here, kid? Thought we agreed it's better not to be seen together in public." Geegee aimed the words at the young man who'd just come in to the Spinners and sat down opposite him

"I heard the police dragged you in, and don't call me *kid*," he complained. "Thought I'd better check that you kept your mouth shut," he whispered back.

There was a time when Geegee would never have stood for cheek like that from anyone but he had developed an unfamiliar respect for this lad. He had ideas, good ones, and he was proving to be a big help.

He stuck a pint in front of Geegee.

"No worries, they had to let me go this morning. They're racing around chasing their tails. Anyway, I've got an ace in the hole." He tapped his nose and coughed.

"You've done what we agreed?"

"Yep, it's all lined up. By tomorrow night we'll have a clear path." He looked at the boy. "You've got things sorted your end? I don't understand what you've done but you're sure it'll work?"

"I'm good," he smirked. "Far better than people around here give me credit for. You're the brawn, Mr Gibbs, the man with the shady contacts, but I'm the brains. I'll have the authorities run ragged wondering what the hell's going on. All we have to do is sit back, watch, and then pick up the pieces — the very lucrative pieces."

"I'm not going to cross you, lad, but I still don't get it. Why would a posh boy like you want to get mixed up with a criminal? You're not having a laugh are you?"

"No I'm not; I'm deadly serious. Surely, I've proved that by now?"

"That's as may be, but it's not normal. People like you don't get mixed up with the likes of me. They don't deal drugs and they don't drink in places like this. Anyway, you can't need the money."

"That's where you're wrong. I've got plans and I need as much as I can get my hands on. Where I'm working at the moment certainly doesn't pay enough."

Geegee laughed again. "You telling me you're short of money, posh boy?" he taunted. "Not getting enough spends?"

"Don't say things like that," came the angry retort. "You wouldn't laugh if you knew the truth," he said with spite. "The job's a real drag. They've got me scrubbing bloody vehicles. Scrubbing and greasing, that's all I do all day."

"You really are hard done by, aren't you, lad? But it's only a stopgap, I'll bet. Some sort of work experience. Soon you'll have a proper job, buy your own house and own some posh car. You're bound to, a lad like you who went to a private school and university."

"Just as well I did those things, because that's what makes me so useful now. And you'd do well to keep that in mind, Mr Gibbs. If this is to work then we need each other, never forget that."

It sounded like a threat. Geegee looked hard at the lad. "Don't try turning the screws on with me, because you'll come off worst."

The young man narrowed his eyes. He looked about to explode.

Geegee realised he'd pushed the wrong button and he'd better watch out. Time to smooth things over. "Look, let's just get the next couple of days done with and go from there. We're both strung out — so much going on." He needed the boy to calm down.

"Like I've said, it'll be okay, nothing can go wrong. The dry run is organised my end. Yours?"

"Everything's set up according to plan," Geegee confirmed.

"This is the first step. After this weekend, all the drugs around here will be supplied by us." His eyes widened. "We're set to make a fortune. We'll have all the power, we'll run the streets. We'll have the money to do whatever we want."

"A guaranteed supply, cheap from the continent, that still what we're aiming for?" Geegee asked.

"That's what I promised."

The lad had done his homework. Geegee could never get his hands on enough, and folk always wanted what he hadn't got. The Hussains had it all sewn up. Currently they were the outfit with the guaranteed supply, theirs came in with the tobacco. What he'd give for an operation like that!

"And it'll work like you said?" He looked at the lad. He appeared keen enough but he was young; he might be bright but he was inexperienced. What could he possibly know about the drug-dealing business? "You'd bring it in on those coaches of Webb's?"

"Yes, piece of cake. The coaches are never checked. This dry run will prove everything I've told you. For example, there's a run to Amsterdam weekly, and I could get you anything you want and cheap too. You'll wipe the floor with the Hussains. There's no way they'll be able to compete."

The boy must have read his mind.

"And we split down the middle, fifty-fifty?"

"That's what we agreed. In a short time I want us to run the whole drugs thing in this town and beyond. The Hussains will be history."

A common bond.

"All we have to do is follow the plan. Everyone does as they're told and it can't fail. We've gone over everything."

Geegee nodded. "Okay, but we shouldn't be seen together until after it's done — could cause talk. Once we know it's gone okay, then it won't matter."

The lad agreed. "I'll be round your flat later to finish up, so make sure you're alone. I'll need to set things up on the laptop."

* * *

"We still need to know why Reader ran. Have we heard from the ports?"

"No, sir, but they have his photo, the recent one, the one we took here when we brought him in," George reported.

"Brenda Hirst's watch has gone to the Duggan Centre," Greco told them. "There may still be traces of DNA on it apart from the three we know about. Professor Batho says it will take a while but it could yield some useful information."

Greco stood by the incident board in front of the team. "Rose Donnelly lived at Alderley House on Link Road. Finding her is now of prime importance."

He could almost see the team groan. He knew what they'd be thinking. That as far as anyone knew she was merely missing and that could be because she'd simply gone on holiday.

"Despite what you all may think, Rose is involved. We know that her phone was used for that last call but there's still no sign of it. We need that phone. It will harbour valuable DNA too. It might be worthwhile searching the canal bank again just to make sure. After all, that's where Gibbs says he found the other things."

"I'll ask uniform to organise it," Grace volunteered.

He nodded. "I don't hold out much hope. There was something not quite right about yesterday." Greco looked straight at Quickenden. "Gibbs should have told us about his alibi straight away but he didn't." He paused. "It was as if he needed time to organise something." He could almost see his sergeant wriggle with discomfort. Something had gone on there, something that could jeopardise the case? He hoped not.

As he spoke, Greco made notes on the board; the latest timeline. He wrote in a neat script, carefully placing one note directly under the other. "I want that pub watching too, and Gibbs in particular."

"Do you want me to see to that, sir?"

Greco didn't reply, he'd got marker pen on his fingers and was staring at it. The ink was black — he'd have to go and scrub it off at the earliest opportunity.

"You mean given that you're always there anyway, Sergeant?"

Quickenden hung his head. "They wouldn't think it odd, me being there, would they?"

"Anything, and I mean anything suspicious and you report back," Greco replied firmly. "We'll also hassle the port, and keep the search for Reader on its toes and we don't drop our guard. Rose is out there somewhere and I want her found."

"We have no evidence that she's not just gone away, sir."

"Not as such, but I doubt that's the case." He looked at Merrick. "The state of her home, the fact her phone is dead, neither of those gives me any confidence that she'll simply turn up with a suntan." He paused for a moment.

"Grace and Craig, try to trace her movements over the weekend. Who saw her, who visited the house, who she spoke to. You never know, someone may recall something. Grace, find out if she used social media."

"A fingertip search of her house might yield something," Quickenden suggested.

"It may come to that yet," Greco agreed. "Now for something totally unrelated." He inhaled deeply. "The bomb scare in Manchester this morning may be the work of a terrorist cell working from here in Oldston."

He fell silent as a barrage of questions hit him.

"You're joking!" Grace looked genuinely shocked.

"We don't know if there's anything in it. But in any event the case isn't ours; it's firmly in the hands of the counterterrorism unit. However, if during the course of any investigation we're involved in we get wind of anything, then we must let the DCI know. Everybody got that?"

The moment the briefing was over, Greco hurried down the corridor to the gents. He spent the following ten minutes with a nail brush and soap until every last trace of ink was gone.

Chapter 14

"It's work, Stace, and easy too," Daz bragged to the young woman. "I'll only be gone for the day, so no biggie. Me and Tan have already got fifty each upfront." He reached in his pocket. "Here." He smiled, fanning out the ten pound notes for her to see. "And there's more when we've done — easy, like I said."

He watched her reach out, biting her lip as she stroked her fingers across the notes. He knew they really needed it— she'd had threats from the gas people and there was no food in the house.

"Is this something you're doing for Kashif, Tan's brother?"

Daz nodded. It'd do no harm to keep the truth from her. He daren't tell her about Geegee.

"You sure, Daz? Cos I don't want you mixing with that toerag Geegee."

"I've not even seen him in days," he lied.

"And it's nothing to do with that copper coming here and that statement thing you had to give?"

"No, Stace, I told you that was about some property I found by the canal. The watch is valuable and there might be a reward," he lied again, "police just wanted the details, that's all."

"So what's it you're doing for Kashif?"

"Nothing much."

"Is it the ciggie run? Is that what you're getting into?"

"Why? What if it is?"

"Because Kashif's trouble, that's why. Sooner or later he'll get caught and he'll drop you right in it."

"That's just fucking stupid. Kashif's too careful. He's got his back well and truly covered. Anyway he wouldn't let Tan do anything dangerous, would he?"

"Whether Tan's in or not, I still don't like it." She shook her head. "I don't like it, Daz; you shouldn't get mixed up in all that. They could get you into all sorts of trouble. You don't want to go back inside. Cos if you get banged up again, then I'm gone," she told him firmly. "And Ben will be gone too," she added, indicating the pushchair in which his two-year-old lay sleeping.

"It's easy money, Stace. A trip to the docks then back to Naz's shop. We'll be fine." If she found out the truth then she'd kill him.

Stacey sighed and started to fold the washing that had been drying on the clothes airer. "So who's going to drive? Not you; you haven't got a licence. Remember?"

Daz shrugged, pulling a face. He'd no idea what to tell her. "I'll sort it," he replied, irritated by her attitude. "Tan will borrow a car off one of his family."

"Well, that's not sorting it because Tan's got no licence either," she snapped at him. "You've got today to get things organised, so do it. You really don't think these things through, do you, thicko!"

His mobile rang — it was Tan.

"Hey, bro, all set for tomorrow are we?"

"Ask him about the car," Stace insisted.

He wandered out through the door and into the hallway where she couldn't hear him. "Stace is giving me grief about the job, so not a word," he warned him. "She mustn't know the truth about what we're doing. If she asks we're doing a ciggy run for Kashif and you are getting us a car." He heard his mate grunt a reply. "How about you? We've got to be at the bus station for nine in the morning."

"Yeah — Kashif don't want me till later so no worries."

"Okay — see you at the stop, and don't be late."

With a bit of luck this could work and Stace need never know the truth.

"So — the driving organised or what?" Stace began to speak the moment he entered the living room.

"Look, this is my first time so I have to go easy. I can't lay down the law. Kashif's sending someone with us to drive," he told her at last. "You mustn't say anything about this, Stace, about me doing the ciggy run, and particularly not to that gobby mother of yours, understand?"

* * *

Greco was sitting at his desk mulling over the statements yet again. He read each one carefully, making notes in his book. "Webb's workshop isn't on the industrial estate, the one near the canal, but it's only a couple of hundred yards away," he said, looking up. "Craig, you took this statement from one of the staff at Webb's office. It's important; you should have flagged it."

"Sorry, sir, I didn't realise."

"Anything we find could hold the key to this," Greco explained. "We've got dozens of statements. We should view them as pieces in a jigsaw. We're looking for how Brenda Hirst got the oil under her fingernails." He shook his head. "It occurs to me that Webb's workshop might be a possibility."

"Do you want me to take a look?" Craig asked. "It wouldn't take long. I'll get an oil sample and pop it along to the Duggan."

"No. Ask a uniformed officer to go instead," Greco decided.

He sighed, rearranging the pens on his desk yet again. He'd have to look through all the statements once more just to be sure. Where one thing had been overlooked there was bound to be something else.

"Call for you, sir," George interrupted, "from downstairs."

It was Sergeant Kendrick, one of their uniformed colleagues. "I'm afraid there's been another body found, sir," he began, "and in more or less the same location as the other one."

Greco felt his stomach tighten. "Male or female?"

"Female, I believe, sir and in a right state."

"Who called it in?"

"A man out walking his dog."

What was the betting that this was Rose Donnelly?

Quickenden had been listening. "Trouble, boss?"

"We need to go, Sergeant — the canal bank. We've got another one."

"You think—?"

"Yes, I do," he nodded. "We should have found her, done more to hone down to the truth. All this about her going away, it clouded the issue."

"We don't know it's Rose, sir."

"True, but Rose or not it's some poor woman who's probably met her untimely end in tragic circumstances." He picked up the phone and rang the Duggan. "Doctor Barrington, please."

"Inspector, how can I help?"

Her voice was light, almost tinkly, with a smile behind it. Suzy used to talk to him like that when she wanted something.

"Will you meet me by the canal, where we found Brenda Hirst? We've got another one," he told her soberly.

"Yes, of course," she replied, her tone somewhat flatter. "Give me twenty minutes or so, and I'll be with you."

* * *

"It's worse this time," Quickenden noted, putting a hand over his mouth. "She's been dead longer, smells a bit."

"It is Rose Donnelly," Greco confirmed. "We've had her photo on the board all week." He turned away. He was annoyed with himself. This should have been looked at closer but they'd been too tied up with the Brenda Hirst murder. Rose had paid a heavy price.

The body was rolled in a white sheet with just the back of the head and a mop of brassy blonde hair visible.

"You still can't be sure. We'll have a closer look when the doctor turns up. For now, all we can really say is that it looks like Rose — well, the hair does."

"You're learning, Sergeant, picking up my habits." Greco revealed a glimmer of humour for a moment. "But we have to be realistic. She went missing at more or less the same time and has been dumped in the same place."

He turned and looked towards the road. Natasha Barrington was late and he could do with getting off; Matilda needed picking up. He was learning fast the restrictions children could put on a job. He just wanted to get suited up and get on. Once he had a good look at the body, then he'd know for sure. After that he'd wait for the post-mortem in the morning. He'd get Matilda and go clear his head.

He looked at the landscape around him. He used to enjoy running. If it wasn't so wet and muddy, the canalside would be a good place to run. When he'd lived in Norfolk he'd jog along the quiet country lanes or around a disused aerodrome near his home, round and round, thinking about nothing in particular. It cleared his head like nothing else and then he could think, think properly.

"Inspector!" Natasha Barrington called out as she locked her car. "A suit for both of you and I've brought the cavalry with me." She gestured at the people carrier that had pulled up with a CSI team in it.

She was suited up and ready to go with the voice recorder primed. "Another one." She frowned. "I'll have a look, give you my initial findings and do the PM tomorrow."

Greco nodded; that was fine by him.

"Female, roughly forty-five to fifty," she said, kneeling down. "Life hasn't treated her well," she noted grimly, peeling the sheet away, "old before her time."

That seemed to be something a lot of the women in this place had in common. Greco moved next to her and hunkered down. The eyes were missing. That confirmed it. "Same killer as before, and it is Rose," he told Quickenden.

"Same killer, it might be, but a different method, Inspector."

The doctor unwrapped the sheet and stared at the abdomen.

"What's that?" Speedy asked, shocked.

"Most of her large and small intestines, Sergeant. But horrific as it looks, this wasn't the cause of death. This was." She pointed to the neck. "Her throat's been cut. She'll have sustained a huge blood loss. It's difficult to say without proper facilities, but I'd say her bowel was removed bit by bit. Death, I would estimate sometime yesterday."

Greco shuddered.

Whoever had taken Rose had wanted her to suffer before he killed her. But why was this murder so different from that of Brenda Hirst? Her death had been quick, but Rose must have been imprisoned somewhere.

"Inspector!" A voice called from further along the bank. It was one of the CSI team.

"We've found this."

He was holding up a potato peeler in an evidence bag. Greco went over for a closer look. The blade was covered in dried blood. He inhaled deeply. It looked like they had found the implement that had been used to take her eyes. A break — if it yielded any evidence such as DNA other than Rose's, or even fingerprints.

"I'll know much more after the PM," Natasha Barrington told them. "And that won't get done until tomorrow I'm afraid. Everything else will go to Professor Batho." She got up and pushed down the hood of the suit. "Thought anymore about my offer?" She smiled.

Greco looked at her. Natasha Barrington was a good-looking woman but he hadn't even considered dating since his split with Suzy. But if he was to put his toe in the water again, she was a possibility. He knew his failings only too well. And to counteract them he needed something else apart from work. Suzy had always said so and all the medical advice he'd had over the years agreed. So should he take her up on the offer? But was he even capable of having another relationship with a woman? Suzy had been his life, both she and Matilda. He'd have to give it more thought, but not here. This wasn't the right time.

"When all this is over." He tried to smile. "When I'm embroiled in a case it takes me over and this is a bad one. I'm not good company, too fixated on catching the perpetrator."

"You're young, Stephen," she said, using his first name for the first time. "You have to learn to let go, live a little. I'm not going to give up. I'll ask again," she promised, tapping his arm.

"Where to now, sir?" Quickenden asked.

"We'll call it a day and see what the PM throws up tomorrow."

"The peeler is intriguing, sir. Why leave it?"

"We have to ask if it was left by mistake or on purpose. Either way, it throws up more questions than answers. We'll discuss it tomorrow."

Greco needed to leave now to pick up Matilda from Grace's mum. His daughter was happy enough with the arrangement but he didn't want to push it.

"I'll drop you at the station and get straight off," he told Quickenden. He knew his sergeant would have no argument with that.

* * *

"I thought we could send out for a pizza," Greco told his daughter. "A bit of a treat, and we could have ice cream for afters."

Matilda Greco jumped in the air and clapped her hands.

"Can I look at the pictures and choose?"

Greco handed her the menu that had been pushed through his door earlier that week and left her perusing it while he checked his emails. Arturo had contacted him again. He'd had another look at his own family history records and found something. The man Greco surmised to be his Italian ancestor, Lorenzo Greco, had left a wife and children behind when he'd absconded. The problem was Arturo didn't know anything else. What Greco needed was proof that the Lorenzo who left Milan was the same man who married in Kent in 1847 calling himself Laurence Greco. The man from Kent had no past. He didn't appear on the 1841 census and there was no UK record of his birth. He sent him a thank-you email and went back to Matilda.

"I want the cheesy one with tomatoes," she told him, "and can I have fries and a drink?"

Greco didn't usually send out for food, and if he did it was unlikely to be food of this variety but he'd had a hard day and it was a treat for Matilda.

"Okay, Tillyflop, I'll ring the man and get it sorted." But before he had the chance, the front doorbell rang.

It was Suzy.

Greco was both surprised and relieved to see her. "You're back quick. I thought you'd be at least a week." He smiled.

"I couldn't stand it a minute longer," she replied, shaking her head. "I'd forgotten what it was like, what they were like, and with dad being ill, it was even worse."

Greco wasn't sure what she meant.

"Mummy!" Matilda said rushing to meet her. "We're having pizza. Daddy's going to ring the man."

"Not like you, Stephen," Suzy said giving him a quizzical look. "What happened to all that guff about healthy eating?"

"A long hard day happened."

"Can I stay and have some pizza with you both? Perhaps you could open a bottle of that expensive wine of yours. I see you're stocked up," she said nodding at the wine rack in the kitchen.

"She can, can't she, Daddy? Then we can all watch telly together."

He nodded his agreement. "But if you drink, you're not going to be able to drive home," he reminded her.

"You're never off duty are you?" She shook her head. "But it's easily sorted. I'll stay here with the two of you. You don't mind, do you?"

He wasn't sure. Where would she sleep for a start? There were only two bedrooms. Suzy was behaving oddly. Since their divorce she had kept him very much at arm's length. Apart from meeting up to take Matilda for the weekend or discuss her welfare they'd had precious little to do with each other. Something was going on but he'd no idea what.

"You look troubled, Stephen. You need to lighten up."

He pursed his lips. Twice within a few hours a woman had said that or something like it to him. "This isn't like you, this casual approach to being with me. Has something happened? Only you're making me nervous," he whispered to her.

"Get those pizzas ordered first," she insisted.

Suzy took Matilda into the bathroom to get her organised for bed. "You can have your bath then get your pyjamas on. By then the food will have arrived."

Once the child was splashing in the bath, she returned to talk to him. "I've made a huge mistake, ruined everything and particularly the two of us," she began.

Greco looked at her. Ordinarily Suzy didn't say things like that, and where their relationship was concerned, blame for its failure had been firmly laid at his feet.

"Are you worried your parents won't cope, is that it?"

"It's not them." She flopped down on the sofa. "They always cope. My mother is a past master at dealing with everything life throws at her. They don't need me; I just get in the way."

"So, the mistake? Enlighten me."

"You, me, us, Stephen." She looked at him. "You can't be happy with the way things have turned out either."

That much was true. The split and the trauma of the divorce had made him even more obsessed and introverted than usual.

"You made all the running, Suzy. You wanted the divorce. You said exactly what you wanted and I went along with it, right down the line. You came here to Oldston. I just followed in your wake."

"Why, Stephen? Why did you follow me?"

What did she expect him to say? "For Matilda of course." He turned away from her penetrating gaze. It wasn't strictly true and she could see right through him.

"Are you sure that's all it was? Are you sure you didn't want to stay close to me?"

"If I'd let you come alone, then you'd have had it all to cope with. You'd have had no one to help, to give you a break from the childcare. I thought you'd appreciate having me to lean on." She was staring at him. What did she want? What did she expect him to say? "Look, Suzy, where's all this coming from? I thought you were settled here, had the life you wanted. To be frank, I thought you'd come here because of some man you'd met," he admitted.

Now she was laughing at him. "A man! Stephen you don't know how funny that is," she told him, "and you call yourself a detective. Do you want to know the truth? It sounds ludicrous now," she said with a light laugh. "It was my parents. I presumed you'd realise that."

Greco was confused. He thought he'd already worked all this out. Suzy had got bored and had found herself someone else, simple as that. Now apparently, that wasn't the case at all.

"You don't look very pleased to learn that I was never unfaithful," she said, sipping on the wine.

"It's not that."

"Then what is it? I don't expect much but I thought you'd have more to say. Give me a smile at least," she teased. "You've not gone and got yourself another woman, have you Stephen?" She waited. "You've only been here two minutes."

"No, of course not, don't be stupid."

"It's not stupid. You're not bad-looking. I've seen the way women look at you. You've got a good job, youth on your side."

"Is Matilda okay?" He asked, checking his watch. "The food will be here any time and she's been in there a while."

"She's fine, she's singing away, can't you hear her? And don't change the subject."

"What is it you want, Suzy?" He was going round in circles and didn't know what to think, what to feel.

"Look, we both know you have issues, the obsessive thing, but have you ever thought that I might have problems too?"

"Issues?" He considered this for a moment. "I know I'm faulty, not professionally, I'm a good cop. But you know that I've always acknowledged that emotionally I'm different," he watched her nod. "The obsessive thing is hard to beat, but I do try. I don't enjoy being the way I am. What problems do you have, then?"

"Claustrophobia, Stephen," she told him pointedly. "Caused by my parent's constant interfering, wanting to run my life, and hers," she said, nodding at the bathroom. "I'd had enough and I couldn't live like that anymore. Something had to change and that was down to me. I tried to talk to you but there was always the job and some case in the way. Do you have any idea how desperate I felt, Stephen? I had to cope with you, your OCD, my parents and their demands, Matilda and my job. I'm only one pair of hands and I couldn't hack it. I was sinking on all fronts and no one even noticed."

"You should have said something."

She ignored that. "At first I thought I'd made a huge mistake in coming up here. To begin with it was too far away from everything I knew. But going back, just for that couple of days and spending time with my parents has made me see that the decision was the right one."

"So what's the problem? Why the change towards me?"

"The mistake I made was in leaving you, Stephen. I know that now and I want to see if we can put things right."

She'd put her cards on the table but he was still out of his depth. He'd had to learn to live without Suzy, to cope on his own. He didn't like it much but he was getting there. Did he really want her back?

"But why choose to live here of all places?" It was all he could think of to say.

"One night after half a bottle of gin and even more wine, I stuck a pin in the map and here we all are."

He couldn't say anything to that. It was just like her. Suzy was so different from him, vibrant, alive, and she took risks — it had been a big part of what made her attractive.

"That's no way to choose your new home."

"I know that now, but at the time it seemed perfectly reasonable. Just be grateful you're not living in the north of Scotland."

She burst into laughter as the insanity of her actions hit home. "I'm a bloody fool; why didn't you stop me?"

"I didn't know how to. But now I wish I had; things would be so very different."

"You don't like it here, then?"

"I'm still making my mind up," he replied.

"I'm sorry; I should never have done it. But I had to get away. I was going slowly mad. But I do regret the way things have turned out. She fell silent. "I was wrong to leave you, to wrench Matilda away like I did, and I want to put things right."

Chapter 15

Thursday

"Your luggage." Daz handed Tanweer a small overnight bag. "The two bags will go in the boot but the rucksack will come on the coach with us. It's got our disguises in it."

His friend nodded. "Who packed the bags?"

Daz shrugged and moved away from the others in the queue. "Don't stress, man, everything's cool. We don't need proper luggage — we're not staying anywhere, remember?"

"But we're standing here with folk waiting for a coach — so if we're not going with them, where are we going?"

"Just act normal and keep your voice down. We'll get off at the first stop — that's a motorway services. We won't get back on, and the coach will leave without us."

"Won't they wonder where we got to?" Tanweer asked, doubtfully.

"Yep, they'll wonder, but there's nothing they can do. After a set waiting time they'll carry on without us."

"I don't get it — why are we doing this?"

"Look, Tan, you and me don't have to get it. We're being paid to follow instructions, being paid by Geegee, remember — so that's what we do, okay?"

Tan lit a cigarette, he needed to think. This was something big; it had to be. "You still haven't said who packed the cases."

"Geegee did, and before you ask I don't know what's in them. I wasn't there and I didn't ask because I'd rather not know."

"He doesn't transport his drugs this way. He doesn't deal in volume for a start," Tan told him as if he knew all about it.

"Geegee could be into anything. I've no idea and I'd prefer to keep out of it."

"So where is it we're supposed to be going on this coach trip we're now part of?" Tan looked round at the other people waiting in the queue.

"According to the tickets it's a theatre break in London, to see a musical. Three nights. Actually the trip sounds quite good." Daz laughed. "It's the sort of thing my Stace would love to go on."

"He's gone to a lot of trouble, hasn't he? And given it's Geegee we're dealing with, that's worrying." Tan had no idea what was going on but it had to involve something really dodgy if that madman was behind it. And given the luggage had been packed for him — well, obvious wasn't it. It was highly unlikely that his pyjamas were sitting in that case.

It didn't take long for the queue to get bigger. Some folk had kids with them, excited kids jumping all over the place and clamouring for sweets from the bus station shop.

"The sooner this fucking coach gets here the better." Daz nudged Tan in irritation. "I could be putting my time to much better use."

145

"Hey — less of the swearing, there are kids here and I certainly don't want my daughter listening to what comes out of your foul mouth."

The little girl had been staring at Daz's expensive trainers and the man moved her so that she was standing behind his back while he tackled the two boys.

"Sorry, mate," Daz replied sheepishly.

"I'm not your mate. Any more of it and I'm telling the driver. I'll get the pair of you banned before we even get started — got it, you idiot!"

His face was flushed with annoyance. "The youth of today can't open their mouths without a torrent of swear words in every other sentence," he told another man.

Tan knew that Daz had a short fuse and was itching to retaliate. At any other time he'd have lost his rag completely and lamped the bloke, but not this time. Tan was poking him in the back, urging him to back off.

"We're supposed to keep a low profile, you said. Now the whole fucking coach will have us clocked," he hissed. "Look — we're both sorry, it won't happen again." Tan tried to smile at their accuser.

The man's response was to take his daughter's hand and lead her away, muttering, "Stupid thuggish behaviour — why in Heaven's name did a pair like that want to come on a trip like this, anyway?"

Fortunately, a few minutes later, the coach arrived. Everyone lined up to give their names and have their luggage stored in the boot. Once their two bags were safely stashed Daz and Tan took their seats.

"So when's the first stop, then?" Tan asked.

"Services near Stafford; we'll have about half hour to get gone."

"What's the plan?"

"We get off and go for a coffee like everyone else, but then we sneak off without being spotted. Well, that's the advice from Geegee so we'd better not cross him," Daz warned. "We do it like he wants, okay?"

"How do we get away? Places like that, they're full of CCTV."

Daz tapped the side of his nose. "The disguises, idiot — in that rucksack down here." He kicked between Tan's feet.

"When we leave, no one will recognise us," Daz assured him.

"Disguises — what sort of caper is this? I still don't like all this cloak-and-dagger stuff. It smacks of something big, and how do we get away from the services?"

"A car has been left for us; I've got the keys." Daz tapped his pocket.

* * *

"No Matilda this morning, sir?" Grace remarked as Greco entered the office.

"Suzy, my wife, is back, so she's seeing to her. We've been talking and we'd still like your mum to have Matilda after school, perhaps a couple of times a week."

Ordinarily Greco wasn't given to explaining himself. He rarely discussed his personal life with the team. But over these last few days he'd come to appreciate that Grace was different, she understood. And it helped, the talking, sharing their problems, it definitely had benefits. He was feeling a little better.

But he could see the disappointment in her face. He might feel happier, but this outcome wasn't what Grace had had in mind. Nonetheless she nodded. "I'll organise it. Perhaps when she has Holly, the two get on so well."

"The Duggan have been on, sir," Craig Merrick interrupted. "Professor Batho, no less, and he said it was urgent."

Greco went to the phone.

"We've fast-tracked the potato peeler," Batho began, "fingerprints first and we've struck lucky. There is one thumb print on the handle and it belongs to a Mr Grady

Gibbs. An individual known to you I believe, as both his prints and DNA are on record."

"Thanks, we'll bring him in."

"Also — I was given a further sample of oil late yesterday sent courtesy of DC Merrick. I'll do my best to get it matched today against that found under Brenda Hirst's fingernails. If our endeavours prove fruitful then I'll ring you."

Greco was dubious. As far as he was aware the man did nothing legal for a living and certainly nothing that involved oil. The print was a break but it was also frustrating. They'd had the individual in custody and had been obliged to let him go. It was small consolation that he couldn't have gone off and killed Rose at that point, because she'd already been dead for a day or two.

"Sergeant!" He called down the room to Quickenden. "We need to bring Gibbs in again. His prints were on the peeler."

Greco watched Quickenden's face fall as the full implication of that fact hit home. What was it the man wasn't telling him? There was definitely something, and it had to do with Gibbs's alibi.

"Right, sir, we could try the Spinners."

"So early? Are you sure?"

"He has breakfast there," Speedy explained.

"You seem to know a great deal about this particular villain, Sergeant. Would you like to explain why that is?"

"I know him of old, sir. He's local, I'm local, that's all there is to it," he shrugged. "He's been dragged in here many times . . ." He thought for a moment, "but never for murder."

"Well, that's what's going to happen now," Greco told him grimly. "We have no choice. We have a print on a weapon. It will be checked but I'll lay odds that it's Rose's blood on the blade."

The rest of the team were flicking their eyes from one man to the other. They knew Greco was no fool. They knew about the card game and Speedy's losses, but Greco didn't. If he found out, and with Gibbs in the cells again, it was highly likely, it'd be curtains for Speedy's career with the force.

"Organise that search of the canal bank," he told Merrick. "Let's see if any other items turn up that the CSI team might have missed."

"They don't usually miss much, sir," Grace reminded him.

"I don't doubt that. This case, however, could be the exception." Greco had his own opinion about what was going on, but at the moment that's all it was — an opinion — so he wouldn't share it. He had a shrewd idea that items were being deliberately left for them to find, but he had no proof.

Quickenden said very little as he drove them the short distance to the pub. Greco had organised backup from their uniformed colleagues in case Gibbs got ambitious and tried to run. "You're very quiet, Sergeant. Anything you want to tell me?"

"Like what, sir?"

"I don't go a bundle on gut reaction but that doesn't mean I'm immune to it. I get the distinct feeling that there's more going on between you and Gibbs than just growing up in the same area."

Quickenden shrugged.

"I'll ask one more time, because if I find out you're lying, if Gibbs tells me you had anything to do with the alibi he suddenly pulled out of the bag, then that's your career, Sergeant."

"I wouldn't be so daft, sir."

"I hope not, because you could lose your job for a lot less," Greco reminded him soberly.

The Spinners was empty. Quickenden looked at Les. "Geegee?"

Less shook his head. "Not been in."

"His flat, Sergeant," Greco barked.

They drove along Link Road; Greco re-directed backup and then they pulled up outside Geegee's flat.

"Which one?"

"He lives on the second floor, number five."

Quickenden banged his fist on the door. No answer.

"Open this door or we will force the lock!" Greco shouted.

Several minutes went by and then a neighbour appeared. "Drunk he was yesterday, so he won't hear you. He'll be sleeping it off."

"Get back up to break-in," Greco instructed Quickenden. But then a dishevelled Gibbs threw open the door.

"What the fuck do you lot want? I'm not receiving guests today." He grinned cheekily. "Not myself; had a skinful and I'm sleeping it off."

Greco wasn't amused. "You're coming down to the station with us, Mr Gibbs. We need you to answer a few questions. "I want this place searching, Sergeant," he ordered.

"For fuck's sake not again! I've not got time to piss about with your lot another day this week, got things to do," he said glancing back at the laptop on the table. "And you don't get in here without a warrant," Geegee said, facing him up. "I know my rights and you can't come in without my say-so."

"Get on the phone and get it organised, Sergeant."

Gibbs gave Quickenden a toothy grin, pointed his finger at him and coughed. What did that imply? Greco wondered.

Gibbs was handcuffed and led away by a uniformed officer.

* * *

After several stops to pick up more passengers, the coach finally pulled into the service station. Daz was relieved — this was tedious; he hated coach travel. He had long legs and there was never quite enough room. The coach was full of kids and they were so noisy he'd reached the point where he couldn't think straight anymore.

The motorway services was packed with people. Daz grabbed Tan's arm and led the way to a coffee counter. He ordered two lattes and made for a table at the far end of the café.

"We need to find somewhere to change," he told Tan.

"Change?"

"Yeah, the stuff I've got in here." He picked up the rucksack and placed it on the table. "The problem is where we go."

"The gents — it's obvious."

"Not with these disguises we can't," Daz grinned.

"Why not?"

"Because I had a sneaky peek, that's why," he told his friend. "We might go in the gents as blokes but that's not how we'd be seen coming out."

"You're having a laugh — what's that bastard given us to wear?"

"Look, sit down, drink your coffee and wait until this place is less crowded."

"Not until you tell me what's in here." Tan prodded the rucksack.

"Wait and see," Daz grinned.

The young men hadn't noticed, but the little girl from the bus station had wandered to their table and was standing beside them staring down at Darren's feet again. "He's got trainers like mine," she told her daddy who was seated two tables further down.

He glanced at them and then came across to pull her away. "Yes, love," he said, leading her back to their seats and handing her a drink. "Don't speak to people you don't know."

"But they're on our coach, Daddy!" She pulled a face. "And his trainers are like mine, except for the sparkles."

Daz watched them walk away, before continuing to outline his plan to Tan. "There's a corridor where the toilets are. At the end there's a door that leads out to a fenced off area at the back. We'll sneak out there and change."

Tan shook his head. This all sounded very weird and he was nervous. The little girl was still looking around and smiling at them. "Cute kid," he said absently, smiling back.

"Just keep your mind on the job. You're attracting too much attention, bro. Stop looking at the kid — at this rate they'll remember us. And we defo don't want that."

Minutes later the child and her dad moved away.

"Time to go," Daz decided.

They darted down the corridor to the toilet block, pushed open the door and went out into the yard.

"No cameras," Daz noted, looking around. He rummaged in the rucksack and handed Darren a plain black garment. It was a burqa. "Just get it on and no smart-arsed comments either. Change and keep it shut."

"I can't wear this!" Tan exclaimed, shaking his head. "You're off your flaming head — you and that crazy Geegee."

"Look, it's just until we get to the car so shut up. Pull it over your clothes, it's plenty big enough."

Daz demonstrated, easing his own garment over his tall frame. It covered him from the neck down to his toes and when he pulled the head-piece into place it left only a narrow slit for his eyes. Darren Hopper had disappeared under yards of black fabric and no one would ever guess his identity. Then he minced up and down the yard on his toes, trying to appear more feminine.

"No chance," Tan protested. "I can't; it's not what men wear."

"You want the rest of the money, don't you? If you wimp out now, Geegee'll do his nut. He'll beat the crap out of you."

Tanweer scowled and shook the thing. He really didn't have much choice. "Hold the other end while I wriggle into it," he complained. "But don't you dare tell anyone what we did, and don't take any photos with that damn phone of yours either," he warned.

"You look fine, we both look fine. No one will know it's us."

"We look like fucking idiots. Look at you, the thing's too short —it's half way up your leg."

"I'll just hunch over as I walk, and stop stressing. We go back down the corridor, past the café, and we're out of here."

This was getting worse with every passing second. Tanweer couldn't understand why it all had to be so convoluted. What the hell was wrong with simply walking to the car in their ordinary clothes?

Daz led the way with Tanweer shuffling along behind him. They got a few odd looks but nothing more.

"The coach driver's over there," whispered Tan.

"He's not going to recognise us, is he, stupid?"

"Some of the others are waiting to get back on — that kid and her dad, look."

"Tan, will you give it a rest," Dan hissed back. "We shouldn't talk, people will guess something's wrong — men in burqas, that's not normal!"

The two strolled past the waiting queue as casually as they could. Tanweer was nervous — about being caught, about wearing this thing, and he couldn't quite get the gait right. He felt as if he was wearing fancy dress, and trying to act like a female was just too damn difficult.

* * *

The little girl spotted them. She was giggling and tugging on her dad's arm.

"It's that man again, Daddy!" She laughed. "The one with my trainers. He's wearing a funny dress now."

He took hold of her hand, and glanced up. She had to be wrong, because all he saw was two Muslim women in burqas. They were heading off towards the car park. They were too far away to make out the footwear but something was wrong. They were big, clumsy-looking and with their long strides, neither of them looked like a woman. Perhaps she was right. So what were those two fooling around at now? he wondered, and if they were fooling around wasn't their choice of garb in bad taste? He'd no idea what was going on, but he'd have a word when they got back on the coach.

But, of course, neither did get back on. Everyone waited patiently for the first ten minutes or so and then the annoyance set in. People were anxious to be off — this was eating into the time they had to spend in London. The man had promised to take his daughter up to Oxford Street to some of the big shops.

A woman made her way to the front and had a few choice words with the driver. He didn't seem sure of what to do. He got off and disappeared into the café, returning minutes later and calling on his mobile.

"Sorry, folks, I've got to give them another twenty minutes," he told everyone finally. "It's the rules, and so I don't have any choice in the matter."

"Are those men naughty, Daddy?" she asked. "Is that why everyone is getting angry?"

Her dad patted her hand and nodded. "Why were they wearing those funny dresses? Have they gone to a party instead?"

She was right — he should have taken what he saw more seriously. Their behaviour was way off beam. What had they been up to that merited such a disguise? It hit him — they hadn't been fooling around, they'd been leaving. They had no intention of rejoining the coach, and if they'd come prepared, brought the burqas with them then this had been planned. A dozen different possibilities thundered through his brain leaving him feeling very uneasy. He had to speak to the driver. "Come with me," he said, taking his daughter's hand. "And bring your stuff."

The little girl picked up her coat and her bag and followed her daddy.

"They're not coming back," he told the driver. "We saw them heading off towards the car park earlier and they were both wearing a disguise. I think we need to get everybody off this coach and call the authorities."

The driver looked at him as if he'd lost his head. "No, mate, they'll have lost track of time," he replied casually. "I've asked them in the station to put out a call on the PA system." He smiled. "Don't worry, they'll be out in a minute and we'll be on our way."

"No, they won't. I've told you, they're not coming back. They planned to do this. But what's more important is that their luggage is still in the boot." This terrified him more than anything. "You must remove it — leave it behind or at least see what's in their bags."

"Don't be daft, I can't do that. It's against the rules," the driver prickled with annoyance.

The man shook his head. He could see that all the driver wanted was a quiet life, a steady run down the motorway system before he had to do battle with the traffic of inner London.

"You have to ask yourself why they'd do a runner like that, and why they'd wear burqas to conceal their identity. Think about it man, they didn't want to be picked up by the CCTV."

"Wear what?"

"They were both wearing a burqa," he explained patiently. "You know, the long garment that some Muslim women wear — covers everything but the eyes."

"Are you sure, mate? You could be mistaken. If they were all covered up, how can you be sure it was them?"

"My daughter recognised the trainers that one of them was wearing." He shook his head, he was losing patience. "Look, are you going to act on this, or what? I think

155

something's going on, and I think you should do something about getting people off this coach and having that pair's luggage examined."

"If you're wrong, I'll look a right fool." The driver shuffled uncomfortably in his seat.

Things weren't moving fast enough. Surely the coach firm must have set procedures in place for an incident like this? He couldn't wait any longer. Taking hold of the microphone the driver used for announcements, he addressed the passengers himself. A few, those who were sitting near the front had already heard everything he'd said and were whispering amongst themselves.

"We've lost a couple of passengers," he began. "They got off like the rest of us but they haven't returned. Instead they've disappeared towards the car park wearing disguises. I, for one, am concerned that their luggage is still here, in the hold. At the very least I want it removed and handed over to someone who can have it examined."

"Bollocks! Let's just get going," a man shouted from the rear of the coach. "We're wasting valuable drinking time holed up in this shit-hole."

The concerned man swore under his breath. They were morons, the bloody lot of them.

"Come on, we're leaving," he told his daughter. "You can give me my luggage; we're definitely not going any further," he told the disgruntled driver.

"But I want to go to the show, Daddy." She tugged at his arm. "I want to stay at the hotel, I've told my friends and everything, and I want to go to the shops."

Tears were welling up in her eyes. He felt really bad about having to disappoint her but something wasn't right here. "We'll do something else, love," he promised her.

He lifted her off the coach steps and set her down on the footpath. The driver was on his mobile again. With any luck he'd be getting some proper advice about what to do.

He was shouting, rubbing his head. Once he'd clicked the mobile off he turned to look at the man who was waiting for him to open the hold. The driver looked flustered and his face was red and sweaty. He wiped it with a hanky. He definitely looked worried now.

"You'll all have to get off," he announced to the other passengers.

There was a torrent of moaning and a great deal of abuse. The man who'd sworn earlier was shaking his fist through the window.

The driver jumped down the steps and indicated for them to stand back. "You can't have your luggage yet," he told them. "They're going to evacuate the building, and then we'll see," he added quietly.

Once everyone was off the coach, he ushered them back to a covered area in front of the car park. People were already leaving the cafe building and making for their cars. Something had obviously happened, but no one had a clue what that was.

"We can go into that building over there to wait," the driver told everyone. "This young man will lead the way and get you all some coffee or something," he said, indicating one of the security staff. "The police are on their way and they'll sort it out."

There was more chatter and complaining from the passengers. "So you're taking me seriously, then?" the man asked the driver, surprised at the sudden change of mind.

"I've got no choice, mate. It's official. There's a bomb scare here in this service station. Apparently one of Webb's coaches has some sort of device on it and we're the only one here."

Chapter 16

Greco gathered the team together first thing. "Doctor Barrington has determined that Rose Donnelly died forty-eight hours ago, so on Tuesday." He looked at them. "I'm going to interview Grady Gibbs. I know what the prints suggest but I still want a detailed run-down of his movements this week, and Tuesday in particular."

"That's easy enough," Quickenden told them. "For most of Tuesday we had him here, overnight too. For the rest of the day he was at the Spinners."

For the moment Greco ignored him. "Rose had been drugged, morphine most likely. We know Gibbs has access to that." He sighed. "What we don't know is where she was kept. He has a flat and that is being searched as we speak. We need to know if he had anywhere else, a lockup, a workshop, anything."

Greco watched Quickenden shake his head. "What is it, Sergeant?"

"Geegee's never gone in for anything like that, sir. The idea of him having a workshop is ludicrous. He's never done any work as far as I know and he wouldn't pay the rent. A lockup? Unlikely; he doesn't deal in anything that would need that much space."

"Nonetheless, if he is our man then he killed Brenda too. So how did he get them to the canal bank and why there? It's fairly well used and whoever our killer is must have known that the bodies would be found quickly."

"I know what this looks like, sir, but this is way off beam for Geegee. Granted Oldston would be better off without him but he's never killed before. If he did, if some fight or other got out of hand, it would be because he'd whacked them too hard. He certainly wouldn't go gouging eyes out."

"His prints were on the peeler. How do you account for that?"

"I have no idea but I still don't think he's our man," said Quickenden.

"Sir," Craig interrupted, "one of the CSI team from Gibbs's flat." He handed Greco the phone.

Greco listened for a few moments then turned to the team. "Rose Donnelly's phone has been found in Gibbs's flat," he told them. "Does anybody have any ideas how to account for that?"

"The evidence is mounting up." Grace nudged Speedy.

"Sergeant, you can interview him with me," Greco decided. "Craig, give Professor Batho a ring and ask if he has anything on the oil yet. Grace, anything on social media?" The oil was another thing Gibbs had going for him, along with the fact he'd been in custody on Tuesday. The two combined might be enough to rule him out.

"No, sir, Rose didn't have a Facebook account, but there might be something on her phone when it's looked at."

"The two of you look at Rose's movements from the last sighting of her. Talk to neighbours, look at any CCTV you can find, work out what she did and who she spoke to. You might want to look up that woman we met the other day at her flat."

"Mavis Bailey?"

Greco caught her eye. She had a look on her face, one he now recognised — the *I knew it was important* look. And she might be right. Grace had been curious about the Bailey woman and her story from the start.

"Yes, her; her story might have some relevance or it might not, but we need to build a better picture of Rose's life."

* * *

"Tell me about Rose Donnelly," Greco began.

He looked at Gibbs; he was lounging back in the chair, his legs splayed as if he didn't have a care in the world. And given the evidence they had to contradict the fingerprints, he probably hadn't.

"Don't know her, no idea who you mean, guv."

"She lived on the same estate as you."

"So — a lot of folk live on the estate, I don't know them all."

"Tell me about the Spinners pub. Did Rose go in there?"

"Like I said, I never met no Rose. Why don't you go and ask her if you want to know so bad?"

"I wish I could, Mr Gibbs."

"Why not, is she your dead 'un?"

Greco didn't reply. "Do you walk along the canal?"

"Don't walk if I can help it," he grinned. "Not good for me. I've got a bad back, you see."

"How've you spent your time this week, Mr Gibbs?"

"In bed, in the Spinners — that's right, isn't it, copper?" He looked at Quickenden who nodded. "And I spent most of Tuesday here, even slept here if you remember."

Greco was well aware of that. Natasha Barrington said Rose had died on Tuesday. He rubbed his forehead. They needed Gibbs to help them. "Get him a coffee," he told Quickenden, and left the room.

He sat at his desk and accessed the interim report about Rose which Natasha Barrington had put on the system. There was no doubt, she'd died on Tuesday. The cause of death was catastrophic blood loss following the severing of the arteries in her neck. Prior to that her abdomen had been opened and her intestines removed, inch by inch. There was also a great deal of morphine in her system, which, given what she'd been put through was probably a blessing. Was Grady Gibbs capable of this, he wondered? His record had him down as a petty criminal and drug dealer. The murders of these two women were way out of his league. He called the Duggan.

"Professor Batho, I have a problem with the Rose Donnelley case."

"In what way, Inspector?"

"The print on the peeler."

"It belongs to Grady Gibbs, there is no mistake."

"I don't doubt it does, Professor, but the problem I have is that I don't think he is our man. Other evidence we have conflicts with that theory."

"On its own the print simply tells you that Gibbs had the peeler in his possession at some time, that he touched it. Whether or not he was the one to remove those women's eyes with it, is for you to determine. There is also the phone, remember, found in his flat. That has his prints on it too."

"Are there any others apart from his?"

"Not on the surface but I'll take the thing apart and check. I'll rush it through and let you know."

Greco went back to the interview room. "Take Gibbs back to the cells for now," he told the uniformed officer. "We'll resume later."

"You can't keep me here, copper. I know my rights. What have you got? If it's a big fat nothing then you have to let me out."

"All in good time, Mr Gibbs," Greco told him patiently. "There will be more questions later. In the meantime I need to keep you here."

"I'll get out, you'll see," he challenged, casting a look Quickenden's way. "I know things, things about him," he nodded at the sergeant. "So if you keep me here I'll talk. What d'you say now, copper?"

"Take him away," Greco told the uniformed constable.

Once they were alone, he told Quickenden to sit down.

"Here, sir? In the interview room?"

"Yes, here, where no one else will hear what's said. What's he got on you, Sergeant?" Straight to the point. Greco was in no mood to listen to any more nonsense from Jed Quickenden.

"Nothing, sir. He's bluffing."

"I'll ask again. What is it he's holding over you? That alibi the other day was dodgy and now this. I think he's blackmailing you."

Greco watched Quickenden wrestle with the decision to confess or not.

"Despite what we've got, the case against Gibbs is floundering. He was here, in custody, at the time Rose was probably killed. A good lawyer will get him off. But we'd be foolish to risk taking this further if he has something on you that he can pull out of the bag whenever things get sticky for him. It could jeopardise any case we make."

Quickenden's face was a picture of doubt.

"I got into a card game and lost, big style," he admitted at last.

"You lost to Gibbs and you can't pay, that's it isn't it?" This was worse than Greco had imagined. What sort of a fool did something like that?

Quickenden nodded. "Craig says he was playing with marked cards. Of course Gibbs denied it. He reeled me in, let me win a little, but now I owe him, and he's using the debt to get his own way."

"His alibi?"

"Wasn't genuine, but he did find that stuff on the canal bank. He didn't take it from Brenda Hirst's body, I'm sure of that."

Greco shook his head. Quickenden could be sure of no such thing. "You're a first-class idiot, Sergeant. If I go to the DCI with this you will lose your job."

"It was a mistake. I didn't have a choice. I know that Geegee is no killer. If I'd thought any different, I would never have gone along with it."

That was something at least, but how to proceed? Greco knew he should take this higher straight away, but he was reluctant to take that step, and he didn't understand why. It wasn't like him.

"What are you going to do, sir?"

"Nothing for now. But you and Mr Gibbs do not come into contact again while he's here — got that?"

Quickenden nodded.

"And this is the very last time I have your back, Sergeant. Do you understand?"

Quickenden mumbled yes, his face white with relief.

* * *

"Inspector, we have found further prints on Rose Donnelly's phone that belong neither to Gibbs nor the dead woman."

Greco sighed with relief. He'd suspected that might be the case, and it could only help his sergeant if the case against Gibbs dissolved into nothing.

"It was worth another look then," Greco noted.

"The phone was an older one, the type where the back can be removed. The prints were on the battery."

"Thanks, Professor, but do we know who they belong to?"

"Nothing on record, but interestingly a laptop computer was removed from Gibbs's flat. It's gone to IT forensics. It's got some complex software on it that's giving them a bit of a headache, but prints on the casing matched the unidentified ones we found on the battery."

That was great work. It would appear that they were now looking for an unknown accomplice of Gibbs. Whoever that was must have visited his flat.

"Who does Gibbs associate with?" he asked Quickenden.

"Anyone in the Spinners who'll give him the time of day," was the reply.

"Who is likely to have visited his flat, spent time there?"

"No one from choice; the place is a dump. Stinks to high heaven, and he has a very unfriendly dog."

"Well, someone has been there recently. They've left their prints on a laptop, Rose's phone and no doubt on other items too. We need to know who that someone is, Sergeant, so I suggest you rack that brain of yours for possibilities."

Chapter 17

"I hate this place," Craig Merrick said as they pulled onto Link Road. "It's never been any different, not even when it was first built. Council filled it full of no-hopers my gran said, and given the trouble it's been to us ever since, she was right."

"I used to live here myself when I was a child," Grace told him with a smile that said, work that one out. "So not everyone on the estate is bad. I turned out alright." She nudged him. "Rose lived in Alderley House, which is here." She pulled up outside. "Mavis Bailey said she lived that way," she added, pointing.

"So what now? We need an address."

"We drive around the corner to the row of shops and then we ask."

"I wouldn't hold my breath. They don't like the police around here."

"Come on, Craig, don't be so pessimistic. We need to speak to the woman. She pushed two grand through Rose's letterbox the other day and I want to know why."

"You've become a proper keen little cop these last couple of days. Trying to impress the boss, aren't you?"

"What if I am. I have no intention of staying a Detective Constable for ever, Craig. I want promotion and that means doing the job right and getting noticed. You should think about it. Stop using Speedy as a role model and get real."

"Speedy's alright."

"Speedy's a bloody fool and he'll lose the lot if he doesn't wake up."

The woman in the newsagents directed them to a house on the outskirts of the estate. It was surprisingly pleasant-looking. The garden was tended and the house was freshly painted. Mavis Bailey was washing the windows as they pulled up.

"Mrs Bailey," Grace said with a smile. "We met briefly at Rose Donnelly's place. I wonder if we could have a chat."

Mavis eyed the two of them suspiciously. "You're police."

They flashed their badges.

"We're from Oldston CID and we're investigating Rose's death," explained Grace.

The woman shook her head. "She was always bound to meet a bad end and it's no more than she deserves. I've heard the rumours. Found on the canalside wasn't she? Her insides hanging out."

The two detectives said nothing.

"They were evil, the pair of them. They deserve everything they get for what they did to that kid. We found him, you know, me and my husband. He's dead now, my Paul, God rest his soul."

"Who did you find, Mrs Bailey? What kid are you talking about?"

"Rose Donnelly and that Gibbs bloke had a kid, about sixteen, seventeen years ago now. They were rotten to him. He was in a shocking state, neglected, abused. The day we found him he must have got out, escaped. He never said, but we reckon that's what must have happened because me and Paul found him wandering along Link Road. He was in shock, terrified, we told the police and he was taken away."

"What happened to the boy after that, do you know?" Grace asked.

"Never saw him again, from that day to this." She shrugged. "They'll have put him into care. He might have been fostered, or even adopted. I hope so, poor little mite."

"And the money? Why would she give you so much?"

"Her idea of a reward, I expect. Not that I wanted anything. It was because we'd found him, the boy — her boy. She'd come into money recently, inherited or won it, I don't know, and I don't care. I want nothing to do with it. Way back then, I'd no idea the boy was hers. That came out years later when she got drunk one night and asked me about him. She wanted to know what I'd done with him, so I told her. I told her about taking him to the police station that day. I did think about going back to the police, telling them who he really was and about her. But what good would it have done? Years had gone by and the boy would have had a new life by then. He'd not thank me for sending that load of rubbish his way again."

"So the money was a thank you for finding him that day?"

"The money was meant to salve her conscience more like," she scoffed.

"What was his name?"

"Liam Donnelly, but I only found that out later, the night she got drunk when Rose asked me about him."

"Why didn't she give the money to whoever took him . . . raised him?"

"Neither of us had any idea who that was," Mavis explained. "Rose Donnelley had no idea who'd brought up her child. I couldn't help her, even if I'd wanted to, because I've no idea either."

"Thank you, Mrs Bailey. You've been a great help."

"I don't see what this has got to do with anything," Craig said as soon as they got back into the car.

"Is that why you were so quiet back there? You need to get stuck in, Craig. Should you find yourself out with the boss again, then try to make an impression."

"I'm not like you. For now I'm happy where I am. Anyway I don't see what Mavis Bailey has to do with anything."

"We'll dig out the records when we get back to the station and go from there. The child was part of Rose's past. We've no idea what happened to him. He could be anyone, Craig, and he might have one almighty chip on his shoulder."

It took George less than half an hour to find the right file on the system. It seemed there had been a child found on Link Road. He'd spent a few hours at the police station and then his mother had claimed him. A report had gone out on the local radio and she'd come forward. That was all the report said. The woman's name was Judith Calf.

"Dead end, then," Craig nodded. "Makes nonsense of what Mavis Bailey told us. Judith Calf wouldn't have got him back if he'd been ill-treated. Mavis must have got mixed up."

"Mavis seemed sure enough to me," Grace replied, thoughtfully.

"I still don't know what it has to do with anything."

"This needs looking at further. If the boy did belong to Rose and Gibbs, then why would a stranger claim him? Whatever is at the bottom of this it might be an idea to know where he is today."

"If he belonged to this Calf woman then he's none of our business."

Grace shrugged, "We just don't know."

* * *

168

"Who'd have a motive?" Greco asked, entering the office.

"Liam Donnelly, sir," Grace announced.

"I take it that's someone related to Rose?"

"From what Mavis Bailey told us, her son — hers and Grady Gibbs's."

"He told me he didn't know her." He shook his head. "Tell me about this boy and his supposed motive."

"According to the report the kid that was found was claimed by a Judith Calf and had nothing to do with Gibbs and Donnelly," Craig reminded them.

Greco scratched his head. "Craig, go and look it up. Find out if Rose did have a son. It shouldn't take long. If she did, then we can find out what happened to him."

Grace gave him a quick rundown of what Mavis Bailey had told them. "If the lad is theirs, then he could have a motive. He could have been harbouring resentment for years."

It was certainly puzzling. Why would a woman claim a child that wasn't hers? But if he was hers, then what had happened to the child Rose had given birth to?

"In the meantime I'm having Gibbs's flat searched," he told them. "The CSI people are there now. Whatever they take away they'll rush through for us."

Greco went through one or two statements and was making notes on the board when Craig rejoined them.

"Rose Donnelly gave birth to a boy, Liam, twenty-one years ago, sir," he confirmed.

"Mavis Bailey was right on that score," Grace said looking up from her desk.

"Oh and Gibbs's brief wants a word," Craig added.

"Who's he got?"

"It's only the duty solicitor but today that's Conrad Hughes." Merrick pulled a face.

Greco hadn't worked at Oldston for long but it was long enough to have had a number of run-ins with Hughes.

"Where is he?"

"Soft interview room, sir."

Greco left them and walked off down the corridor. He had a lot to think about. They needed to find Liam Donnelly and speak to him. Grace should go and talk to Mavis Bailey again and firm up her story about Rose and the child she'd found. In the meantime he had Conrad Hughes to deal with.

Whatever Hughes threw at him he wasn't about to let Gibbs go. Like Quickenden, he doubted Gibbs was the killer but he had a shrewd idea that he knew who was.

"Inspector!" Hughes greeted him with one of his smiles — the one that didn't reach the eyes. "I have to insist that you let my client out of here."

"Your client is holding back valuable information," Greco told him. "I need him to talk to me, candidly; perhaps you'd like to advise him of that. I'm looking for a cold-blooded killer, so Gibbs stays here."

"I hear what you say, Inspector. Speak to Mr Gibbs one more time but if he can't help, then he must be released."

"Won't help, more likely," Greco corrected. "The man takes a perverse pleasure in keeping information from the police. Information that we badly need, Mr Hughes."

"Rubbish. He knows the score."

"He knows the system and how to use it, you mean."

"Sir!" Craig Merrick came into the room. "You're needed."

"I'll let you know when I'm ready to resume with Mr Grady. In the meantime I suggest you go back to your client and advise him to be more helpful."

He turned to Craig, "What is it?"

"The DCI, sir — and the Super."

It must be something major to tempt Superintendent Wilkes down from the top floor. Greco would have to see what was so urgent but first he needed to wash his hands. He'd been in the same room as Gibbs and the man was a mess. After several minutes of scrubbing Greco walked along to DCI Green's office, where the two men sat at the desk.

"Come in, Stephen, and close the door behind you."

Major, then, and not for general consumption.

"You've been made aware of the terrorist cell in Oldston?" Superintendent Wilkes asked.

Greco nodded.

"We've had a warning. One of Webb's coaches, currently parked up at a motorway services near Stafford, has an explosive device aboard. You know the firm, I believe?"

"Inasmuch as the first victim in our current case worked there," Greco replied. "Was the warning similar to the one we had about the shopping centre?"

"Yes; delivered by email and the language was similar."

He said nothing but Greco knew that sending out warning messages wasn't the method terrorists currently favoured. They tended to strike first and claim credit afterwards.

"Do we have a passenger list?" DCI Green handed him a sheet. Instantly he saw the name *Darren Hopper*. "There is a Tanweer Hussain on here," he commented, ignoring the obvious one. "Is he a member of the tobacco smuggling Hussain family?"

"Yes, he is," the DCI nodded. "But they won't be smuggling anything anymore. A team have been sent from Central to bring in Kashif, and the younger brother, Arif. Tanweer will be apprehended once we find him. He and Darren Hopper absconded from the scene and disappeared onto the motorway system."

"So they were working together?"

"We reckon so. They left the café area wearing disguises — burqas, would you believe?"

"What do you want from my team, sir?"

"Both men live in Oldston. They could well come back, so tell your people to keep their eyes skinned."

"How are your enquiries going with regard to the murders, Stephen?" the super asked.

"We're getting there, sir. I'm about to interview a suspect now, actually. The forensic evidence is building, so I'm hopeful." Not strictly true, but it would have to do for now.

He decided not to say anything about Hopper providing Gibbs with an alibi. That could mean getting into boggy ground where Quickenden was concerned. For reasons Greco couldn't quite rationalise, he wanted to protect him if he could.

"Grace, are you ready?" he asked as he entered the main office.

"Yes, sir, but the Duggan have been on. Professor Batho would like to speak to you."

Greco sat at his desk and rang him.

"Inspector, my team have removed several items from the flat of Mr Gibbs. More prints have been found — matching those on the phone and the laptop, and also a set belonging to Darren Hopper. The laptop is interesting for a number of reasons. From our point of view I shall swab the keys for DNA other than that of Mr Gibbs but it's the software that has our IT people intrigued."

The fact that Gibbs had a laptop, at all, surprised Greco.

"Is your suspect computer savvy? Would you say he has the intelligence to set up complex software?"

"Intelligent, after a fashion, I suppose . . . I'm sure he has developed an entire arsenal of nefarious skills honed over a lifetime of criminal activity. Plus the ability to deliver a razor sharp verbal jab. But apart from that he's not the most educated, no."

"The laptop uses the Tor network. We're struggling to find out anything at all. For example, what websites were accessed, what email was sent and received."

"Tor. So there's nothing left for the Internet Service Provider to tell us about?"

"That's about the size of it. So the question is, what was your Mr Gibbs up to in the flat of his?"

"Thank you, Professor, I'll be sure to ask him."

Greco replaced the handset and nodded at Grace. "Time to speak to Gibbs. I hope he's in the mood, because the list of questions has just got longer."

* * *

"You get me out of here; I don't care what it costs," Geegee barked at Hughes. "I've got stuff to do, folk to see and this is pissing me off big style."

"They have nothing, so relax. I'll have you home in time for tea." The solicitor smiled.

"Here we go." Geegee nudged him as Greco and Grace walked into the room. "Speedy running scared?" he jibed at them both.

"Tell me about your friends, Mr Gibbs," Greco said as they sat down.

"Waste of bloody time unless they can do something for me." He grinned.

"Who have you had in your flat recently — say during the last week?"

"No one."

"We both know that's not true. A number of fresh prints have been found — Darren Hopper's for example."

"Oh yeah, forgot about him; he was with me when I found that watch. He must have come back to my place then."

"Who else? Because there is someone, someone who knows about computers."

Geegee eyed Greco with suspicion. They must have the laptop. The lad had said they'd get nowt, that they could examine it until the cows came home but they'd never crack it. He'd told him to keep his gob shut about anything he'd seen. Geegee hoped he was right.

"No one," he insisted with irritation. "Look, you got anything or what?" He nudged his solicitor. "Come on, earn your bloody money. I want out of here."

He gave Greco a resentful look. This bastard was getting too close. He needed to talk to the lad. "Sometimes folk come back after a session in the Spinners. I don't know who, I sometimes have to be taken home."

"See? My client is trying to help," Hughes insisted. "So charge him or let him go."

"Come on, copper, you heard the man. You've got nowt but a few prints and a knackered laptop."

"Why is it knackered, Mr Gibbs?"

"I can't use it, can't make it work properly."

"So you maintain that it's broken?"

"That's it, yeah."

"No, it isn't, Mr Gibbs. Your laptop is heavily protected, and it uses software deliberately engineered to stop people prying into what you do online. Why is that?"

Geegee squinted at him. He'd no idea what the lad did on the thing. But whatever it was, it worked, that's all he cared about. Occasionally he'd use it, if the kid said so. But he was always given exact instructions, told what to key in. The kid had assured him that they needed it to ensure that the drugs came in. That he used it to contact his dodgy friends in Amsterdam. Also that he was using it to plan a neat little scam to get rid of the Hussains. "Don't know about that. It's as it came out of the box."

The copper was staring at him. Geegee could see from his face that he didn't believe a word, but what did it matter? Without cracking that laptop they had nothing, that's what the lad would say.

"Okay, Mr Hughes, your client is free to go," Greco declared.

Chapter 18

It was late afternoon. The team were standing around the incident board watching Greco as he drew a diagram.

"Brenda Hirst — her only link to any of this and to Gibbs in particular, is the watch. Rose Donnelly; her link to Gibbs is much stronger. They had a child together but hadn't had contact in several years. The two women didn't know each other but Rose's phone was used to make that last call to Brenda." He drew a series of lines to illustrate all this and stood back. "It's likely that whoever killed Brenda took her phone. Is Gibbs at the centre of this or are we missing something?"

"Granted he knew Rose, but he had no reason to kill her, sir," Quickenden spoke up. "He's rough, he deals dope and he'd prefer to fight rather than talk but he's getting on these days. In my opinion he's beginning to lose his edge. This," he gestured to the board, "is way off for him."

"And that is the problem. If we're looking at Gibbs, then we're short on motive."

"Too late now, anyway, we've let him go, sir," Grace reminded them all.

"I had no choice. His brief was right; we have nothing concrete, nothing we can take to the CPS."

"We're missing something, sir." Craig was always ready with the obvious.

Greco tapped the centre of the board. "Yes I know. It's not Gibbs who belongs here but someone else." He looked at them all. "So what is this all about? It has become apparent that Gibbs has an accomplice. Fingerprints were found on the phone, the laptop and all over the flat. Anyone got any ideas? Speedy, you're always in the pub. Who does he talk to? Have you remembered any friends he might have enticed back to his place?"

"The boss just called Jed Speedy," Grace whispered to George. "He's mellowing." She smiled.

"He drinks and he plays cards with the usual crew," Quickenden replied. "They're a rough lot, the whole bunch of them. The thing with the laptop, what's that all about? If Geegee could use it, then it'd be to watch porn."

"A high-end laptop was found in his flat. It uses Tor software. We've no idea what it was used for because Tor makes everything anonymous. Whoever set things up made no mistakes and did a thorough job."

"Not Geegee, then." Quickenden shook his head. "He can barely read."

"So who is it that's helping him, and why?" Greco paused, looking at them then back at the board. "You know what this looks like to me? It looks as if someone is setting Gibbs up. I don't do gut feelings, I prefer proof, but I've had the feeling for some time that evidence is being deliberately planted for us to find. The phone in Gibbs's flat, the watch on the canal bank, someone wants him implicated."

"Why, sir?"

"Someone wants him out of the way. Him, Rose and Brenda, though I can't see where she fits into all this."

"The Hussains, sir?" Quickenden suggested. "Because of the drugs. Geegee gives them a lot of aggro. Perhaps they've decided to get rid once and for all."

"That might fit if it wasn't for Rose and Brenda. Why would the Hussains want both women dead?"

"To throw us off the scent," Craig said.

"We'll see." Greco wrote the name 'Hussain' on the board. "Kashif and Arif Hussain have been brought in. An explosive device has been found on one of Webb's coaches. It pulled into a motorway services and was discovered there."

"Why would the Hussain family involve themselves in something like that?" Quickenden asked.

"I believe Kashif has radical leanings."

"He's an overweight windbag, sir. He likes attention and his ranting draws in the youth. He needs them, he supplies them, he makes a lot of money. He isn't going to risk all that."

The office phone rang and Grace answered the call. "The DCI for you, sir."

They waited in silence as Greco listened. Once he'd finished he shook his head and looked at the team. "Kashif and Arif Hussain have been released. They were kept for less than an hour, it seems. As their lawyer so rightly said, we have nothing on them. It's Tanweer we need." Greco narrowed his eyes. "George, have a look at what we have on Kashif. I want to know where the rumours about him came from."

"Sir," Grace said thoughtfully, "we still don't know what happened to the child Gibbs and Rose had together. Perhaps it's time we found out."

Greco nodded. She had a point.

* * *

Once he got out, Geegee made straight for the Spinners. He had a pounding head and needed a drink. He lit a fag, took a long hard pull and staggered off in the direction of the pub. A couple of stiff whiskeys would sort him out. After that he'd find the kid, see what was going on. "That lad been in?" He scowled at Les, who gave a high-pitched whistle.

"What the fuck happened, Geegee? You look grim."

"Bloody coppers happened, mate. Kept me in and asked a lot of stupid questions. Couldn't make owt stick though so they had to let me go — again. They've got me mixed up with some murderer. Just give me a large whiskey. I need to get the taste of them cells out of my gob."

"Would that be about the bodies found on the canalside?"

Geegee cleared his throat and nodded. "Got nowt to do with me, any of it."

"No one's been in," Les said, placing a chunky glass on the counter in front of Geegee.

"Get me another," Geegee said, as he downed it in one.

Geegee shuffled off to a table and sat down. He was in no mood to talk. He was confused about what had happened. He was protecting the lad, but should he? If he gave any hint that he was going back on the deal then he'd have him. He wasn't going to take the rap for some geeky kid with big ideas. He should get back to his flat. The dog would need sorting and the police were bound to have wrecked the place. "If the lad comes in here, then hang onto him," he barked at Les as he was leaving.

"How do I do that?"

"I don't care how you do it. Knock the bugger on the head and put him in the cellar if you have to."

It wasn't far from the Spinners to his flat. He could hear his dog barking as he started up the stairs. He'd been right — the place was a mess. They'd rummaged through every drawer and cupboard and had left his stuff all over the place. The laptop was gone. He bit his lip. He could only hope that the kid was right and what they'd done couldn't be traced.

He couldn't be bothered with the tidying up. He went to the fridge and helped himself to a can of beer. Stuff the lot of them. He was going to put his feet up and get stoned. If anyone wanted him they'd have to wait until tomorrow.

* * *

"You're back with us, Mr Gibbs. Sorry for doing that, but a dose of sedative was the most expedient way to keep you quiet."

Geegee tried to get out of the chair. He'd been drugged and in his own home too. The little bastard had pumped him full of dope. He couldn't remember letting him in and he'd no idea how long he'd been out.

"What're you doing?" Geegee asked, rubbing his eyes.

"Tidying up. I have to do something before you crack and tell them everything. It hasn't gone unnoticed, you know, that the police seem very fond of you just recently."

"They're trying to pin stuff on me. Murder, would you believe." He tried to laugh but his head hurt.

"I know what they're trying to do. But they've got it horribly wrong."

"I know that too but the new bloke they've got won't let up."

"They've got Rose now, that'll be why. I had to let her go; she was starting to pong a bit."

Geegee had no idea what he meant.

"You don't know who I'm talking about, do you? I'm talking about Rose, your Rose. Surely you must remember her. You used to live together way back when."

He bent down close to the man. "But why should you? You haven't seen her in years. Dropped her like a brick when she took to drinking too much. Shame she had to miss you, though," he whispered, "it would have been some reunion. The two of you were big mates back in the

179

day, remember? I wanted to keep her for longer, let the pair of you get reacquainted but it just wasn't practical. When I'd finished she had a bloody big hole in her guts." He laughed out loud. "I was hoping to drape them from a beam at my place but they kept snapping. In the end most of her bowel ended up dangling on the floor. Quite a mess, you should have seen it."

"You're a bloody nutter." Geegee sniffed in disgust.

"I know that, Mr Gibbs. I've never been any different. Result of a botched childhood. People think I'm nice, generally they like me, but that's a big mistake. You made that mistake, Mr Gibbs. You like me . . ." He laughed again. "Well, you trust me. You were more than happy to let me into your life, to venture into the drugs business with me, and that was another big mistake."

He strutted proudly over to the man in the armchair. "But you can hardly point the finger and call me *nutter*, can you? Because I'm exactly as you and that bitch made me." His face was now only centimetres from Geegee's.

"Nutter," Geegee repeated with venom. "You're nothing to do with me. Until a few weeks ago I didn't even know you."

"But you did, Mr Gibbs. I was in here." He tapped his head. "Or I should have been. Look closely. Are you sure that I'm not just the tiniest bit familiar? Have you never looked at me and wondered, just for a moment, if I could be him?"

"Piss off. You're a proper head case."

"You've no idea, have you?" He shook his head. "You're as clueless as she was. Not very flattering, that. I felt sure that one of you would twig."

"I'm nothing to do with her," Geegee sniffed again. "I didn't even know her."

"Now that does surprise me, it really does, particularly as the pair of you was shacked up in that flat of yours at one time."

* * *

He watched Geegee's face cloud over. Could that booze and drug-addled brain work it out?

"Come on, try harder," he urged. "You must remember. You, her, that poky little flat on Link Road, the tart you got pregnant, the kid you had."

Now he could see a glimmer of recollection begin to creep over Geegee's face as the cogs of his memory rolled backwards. "I think you're getting it at last, Mr Gibbs."

"You're him!" Geegee said incredulously as the penny dropped. "That kid, the lad we had, all grown up."

"No thanks to you," he spat back in his face. "I could have died; no one would have noticed or even bothered."

"You look okay to me. You've done alright for yourself, anyone can see that."

"Looks can deceive," he retorted. "I'm like you said — a proper nut job, and that's down to you, you and that tart I butchered."

"Not us, we did nothing wrong."

"Did you never wonder what happened to me? Did you never search, tell the police that I was missing?"

Geegee shrugged. "She didn't seem bothered, and she was the boss."

"I suppose I shouldn't be surprised, not really. Neither of you were ever concerned about me while I was in your tender care."

"We did our best."

"Your best! I was neglected, half-starved and dirty. Most days you filled me full of dope and hired me out to your paedo friends. How do you think I felt, Mr Gibbs? Me, a small child, unable to defend myself, terrified, having to stand my corner against all those mad perverts? Your idea of 'care' was to make as much money you could out of me and to hell with the consequences."

"It was her idea!" Geegee was screaming now. "Rose was responsible, not me. It had nothing to do with me. We needed money for the rent. We had to do something to keep a roof over our heads. She was always on at me, she was. She never wanted you. You weren't right at birth. They wanted to take you away, but I said we could cope."

"Why? What was wrong with me?"

"You had some sort of syndrome. She was on heroin and drank too much, so you were addicted too."

* * *

Geegee felt weird. He wasn't tied up but he could still barely move. The kid had given him something, but what? "We can talk this through. We've already made a start; things are going okay, so we need to stay close. Things will be happening soon. We need to be ready."

"Oh, things are moving, Mr Gibbs. The Hussains have been arrested. The coast is now clear for whoever has the balls to take over. Soon there is going to be a new drug baron on this block. A hard bastard who'll take no shit off anyone — me," he said jubilantly.

"And me. We're partners. We planned this together."

"You're an old has-been. Why would I want anything to do with you?"

"For old time's sake." Geegee's voice was raspy; his breathing had become laboured and his chest felt tight.

"It's the old times that made me like this. My head's all messed up because of what you both did to me. In the end I had to get rid of Rose," he said at last. "I couldn't stand seeing her day after day. She was a mess. She'd no idea who I was. She turned my stomach so I slit her throat."

"You mean you're a cold-blooded killer?" Geegee's vision was blurred and he felt sick. This was the stuff of nightmares! He'd have been better off staying at the nick.

"Yes, I am, and I enjoy it." The lad smirked, standing over him and for some reason holding a potato peeler in his hand.

Geegee watched as he raised it above his head, shrieking as he stuck it right in front of his eyes. "Recognise this?" said the lunatic. He shook it in front of his face. "It's one like yours, like the one I took from your drawer on one of my visits to your flat." He laughed. "How does it feel, Mr Gibbs, to be played, fitted-up and made to dance to someone else's tune?"

"What do you mean?"

"This, the watch and Rose's phone, they've all got your prints on them. The police know; that's why they dragged you in."

Geegee was nervous; the lad was out of control. "What are you going to do with that?"

"I'm going to take out your eyes, Mr Gibbs."

Geegee screamed, but he still couldn't move — it'd be the drugs.

"I took Rose's eyes."

Geegee couldn't believe what he was hearing. He'd carried out this horrific act and he could talk about it so casually? Geegee was terrified, a feeling he was not familiar with. The boy was mad, there was no doubt about that now.

"Despite everything her eyes are lovely. Look." The boy held out a little box and opened it.

Geegee couldn't believe what he was seeing. He screamed again.

"So blue, so shiny. Just perfect, in fact. Brenda's were brown. Oh, you don't know Brenda, do you? Never mind, I won't have time to explain about her. I'm after something a little more unusual for next time, perhaps hazel or even green. What colour are your eyes, Mr Gibbs?" he asked the petrified man. "I knew a girl at school who had red hair — she had green eyes — wonder what happened to her . . . ?"

Geegee watched as he took a sheet from the bed and spread it on the floor. "You should have tried harder, Mr Gibbs, but you are too much like Rose. Neither of you could amuse me for long. You're like all the rest, a waste of bloody time."

"What are you going to do with me?"

The young man looked at Geegee long and hard and then smiled. The smile seemed like that of a young innocent.

"I'm going to kill you, Mr Gibbs."

Chapter 19

"Kashif and Arif Hussain were taken to the Central Manchester Station for interview. They have agreed to allow their home to be searched and all IT equipment to be thoroughly scrutinised. It will take time, but if they are involved in terrorism, then we'll soon know," DCI Green told Greco later that afternoon. "We couldn't hold them. The arrests were a gut reaction on the part of Central. There is no evidence to link any of the Hussain family to the bomb scare, other than Tanweer. A description of him and his friend have gone out — they've nowhere to hide. It'll only be a matter of time before they're picked up."

"Darren Hopper, the young man with Tanweer, has been to Gibbs's flat. When he's apprehended I'd like the opportunity to speak to him," Greco said.

"Okay, I'll let you know," the DCI agreed. "Are you saying that Gibbs could be involved too?"

Greco shook his head. "I doubt it, but they do know each other, watch each other's backs."

"Where is Gibbs now?"

"I had to release him — not enough evidence," Greco admitted. "He's involved somewhere along the line but he's no longer the prime suspect."

"So who is?"

"Currently we haven't got one. We've followed every lead, weighed up everything we've got, but I still can't see what this is all about."

The DCI wasn't best pleased with the news but it was no good holding back. Things were what they were and Greco wasn't going to dress it up.

He needed something, a break. The case had stalled. Back in the incident room the team were hard at it.

"I've looked at the electoral roll for the time the boy was found wandering, sir. There is no Judith Calf on it," George told him.

"We don't know for sure that that particular child belonged to Rose, do we?"

"Mavis Bailey said that Rose asked about him some years later. Why would she do that? Mavis recalls the original incident vividly. The boy was in a right state. It upset her and she never forgot it. When Rose asked about him, Mavis put the pieces together and realised who he was."

"The police records from the time, do they tell us anything?" he asked George.

"Very sparse — the woman's name and that of Mavis Bailey, nothing else."

Greco wrote the name 'Judith Calf' on the board.

"Sir, that bomb scare at the service station on the M6 involved one of Webb's coaches. Bit of a coincidence that," Grace noted.

Greco stood and thought for a moment. She was right. He wrote 'Webb's coaches' on the board and circled it. What, if anything, was their part in all this? "Rose Donnelley had nothing to do with Webb's, sir," Craig Merrick reminded him.

"Do we know how many people work there, in the workshop?"

"A handful, that's all. They have two full-time mechanics, an odd-job man and currently the boss's son, Nathan, is working there."

"Have we spoken to them all, taken statements?"

"We have, sir. All movements have been accounted for and they work together so it would have been spotted if someone was missing."

Greco's mobile rang. It was Julian Batho.

"Inspector, the laptop we retrieved from Mr Gibbs's flat," he began. "Our IT people have managed to retrieve some of the data. They have reported that it was used to send both of the recent bomb scare warnings that originated in Oldston."

"Are they sure?" Greco was shocked. If they found anything he'd expected it to be about drug dealing or guns; never once had he considered terrorism.

"They are quite sure, Inspector. It isn't much, just snippets of the emails sent from that laptop. Something was planned via that machine. It will be passed on to the counterterrorism unit and they will work on it further. I will keep you posted." There was silence for a few seconds. "I have told you, Inspector because it relates to the case but I have been advised that, for the time being this is privileged information. It might be wise to keep this detail to yourself. I'm sure your superintendent will pass over this information when he's ready."

"In that case, shouldn't you keep quiet too?"

"No, I think you need to know. The case you're working on is difficult enough, without not having all the facts. It's how I work. I am a forensic scientist. I use science to get answers, not to enable others to keep secrets."

Keeping this quiet could be difficult because it meant that somehow the bomb scares were linked to the murders. However Gibbs still didn't fit the bill as a likely suspect. He was a drug-dealing thug not a terrorist. Then again, he was a known associate of Darren Hopper's, who was complicit in planting the device.

"We're going out, Constable," he decided once he'd finished with Batho and thought about the implications of their conversation. "We'll go and visit Mr Gibbs again. He either speaks to us candidly this time or we'll hand him over to Central," he told Craig. Thankfully Craig Merrick didn't ask questions. He simply grabbed a set of keys and made for the car park.

This was getting tedious. Again they were hammering on Gibbs's door and again he wasn't answering. They could hear the dog whimpering behind it.

"That's not right, sir," Craig told him. "The animal's a brute. He doesn't normally make noises like that."

"Break it down, Craig," Greco decided wearily. "There should be something in the boot of the car."

Craig Merrick was a strong young man and with the aid of a crowbar he soon had the flimsy front door open. The flat was more or less as the CSI team had left it. Gibbs was obviously not house-proud. The sheer disorder of the place bothered Greco. He could never understand how people could live like this. He went into the bedroom, which was off the main hallway, while Craig went into the lounge. Greco had expected the man to be comatose in his bed but he wasn't.

"Sir!" Merrick shouted out. "He's in here."

What now? Merrick sounded unhappy.

"He's had it, sir. We're too late."

Grady Gibbs was lying slumped back in an old frayed armchair. His throat had been cut and his eyes were missing. This was the work of their killer — but why Gibbs?

* * *

"The method is the same as with Rose Donnelly," Natasha Barrington confirmed. "Although there are no wounds, other than the throat and the eyes. No attempt at torture this time." He watched her shiver. "I'll do the PM. The report will be on the system later this evening." She smiled at Greco. "I'm working late. Not my usual practice but I need to catch up." She looked at him, the smile still hovering on her lips. "Unless I get a better offer," she suggested. "What d'you say? Fancy that drink yet, Stephen?"

Greco took her arm and led her into the hallway, he didn't like this on-the-job flirtation. "Perhaps I should have said something," he whispered. "My wife is back. Nothing is settled but it wouldn't do to take out another woman, not while there's still a chance."

"Your loss." She tapped his arm. "But the best of luck anyway. Divorce isn't pretty; I know that from my own experience."

"You're divorced too, then?" The question was out before he could stop it. He didn't usually ask such personal questions of relative strangers.

"Yes, a couple of years now. I was married to a fellow doctor. There were lots of reasons why it didn't work. Work was a huge factor, that and too many pretty nurses."

"I'm sorry, I didn't mean to pry."

"Pry away, Stephen, I really don't mind," she said lightly. "I prefer things to be open from the start. Still, if there's a chance you can put things right with your ex then you should go for it. If things go wrong, you can always take me up on that offer of a drink. People like to gossip," she gave him a knowing look. "There are rumours; folk around here have you down as the male equivalent of the ice queen."

"Rubbish. I don't know anyone in Oldston well enough for them to have formed any sort of opinion about me."

"Exactly the point. How long have you been here, a few months? And during that time you've done nothing but work. You've never been to the pub with the lads, or been seen in any bar. You don't go to restaurants. Like I've said before, you need to get out, be seen around the town, dispel the rumours. Whether you like it or not, you are part of this community now and you have to fit in."

Was she right — possibly? He was far too fond of his own company. When he finished work he liked to listen to music, read a good book and go over the day's work. He wasn't naturally sociable.

"You could be right. If me and Suzy make it, I will take her out, show her off."

"Do that. I'd quite like to meet her."

* * *

"There's not much we can do here," Greco told Craig. He checked his watch.

"Back to the station, sir?"

Greco nodded. He was silent for much of the ride back. He was trying to work things out. Brenda and Rose went missing at roughly the same time. Gibbs knew Rose; he didn't know Brenda. Gibbs used Hopper as an alibi for possession of the watch, and Hopper was one of the two who put the device on the coach — a Webb's coach. Someone went to Gibbs's flat, used the laptop and most likely planted Rose's phone. Had that someone also planted the potato peeler; first ensuring Gibbs's print was on it? One way or another someone had gone to a lot of trouble to incriminate Grady Gibbs, but why? What was the motive?

Back at the station he gathered the team together.

"We'll go over everything," he said, once they were seated in front of the board. "Grace, you reckon that Gibbs and Rose knew each other years ago?"

"Yes, sir, and they had a child, one Liam Donnelly," she said, with certainty.

"Do we know if Gibbs and Rose saw each other recently?"

"It doesn't seem so," Grace said. "They led separate lives. I have checked all the sightings of Rose. From what

I've been told, she was last seen at about five thirty on Saturday afternoon."

"More or less the same as Brenda. Both women are taken, Brenda ends up dead pretty quickly but Rose is tortured before she's killed. An attempt is made to seriously incriminate Gibbs and then he's killed. Can anyone suggest a motive?" He'd asked the question, but niggling at the back of his mind was the terrorism thing. It was important but where did it fit in?

"They wanted him incriminated," Craig said.

"Didn't work though, did it? We kept dragging Gibbs in but nothing stuck, and that was down to the evidence. There was too much that conflicted with everything that was planted. They really wanted Gibbs to take the rap for murder, and when that failed they had no choice but to kill him," Quickenden suggested.

"They didn't want him incriminated for just any murder though, so why Rose? Why not one of his gambling buddies from the pub?"

"Because whoever our killer is, sir, he wanted them specifically," Grace suggested.

It was a good point. A killer whose target was both Gibbs and Rose — so who knew them both? Lots of people in this town probably. The real question was, who knew them as a couple?

"So we're back to that link again." Greco looked at Grace.

"So who is this person? Who would want both Rose and Gibbs dead?"

"And Brenda Hirst, sir," Grace reminded him.

That comment was met with blank looks. No one, including Greco, could work out how she fitted into all this. "It had to be someone Gibbs knew and knew well. This someone has gained his trust recently, become a friend."

"Geegee didn't have friends, not from choice he didn't. I mean, who'd want to be friends with that thug?"

Quickenden rolled his eyes. "People tolerated him, played cards with him and were happy to buy his drugs, but that was it."

Greco was thoughtful for a moment. "Recently that changed. Someone has deliberately targeted Gibbs. Got to know him well enough to be allowed into his flat — to use that expensive laptop."

"That's another thing. What were they using it for, sir?"

He didn't answer. Until Tanweer Hussain and Darren Hopper turned up, Greco was keeping what he knew about that to himself.

"Perhaps Gibbs got scared," Craig suggested, "felt pressurised."

"Believe me, people, Geegee doesn't do scared — he loves violence, laps it up. He's sooner talk to you with his fists than waste breath on conversation."

"Who or what haven't we looked at yet?" Greco looked around at the puzzled faces.

"Their child, Liam Donnelly," Grace said with a shake of her head. "He is the only link between Gibbs and Rose that I can see."

"The oil samples might tell us something," Craig suggested.

"Darren Hopper — we need to speak to him," Quickenden added.

"Okay, that's our list," Greco decided. "Who can stay — make a start?" He saw Grace look up at the office clock, it was gone five. "Leave if you must, Grace," he told her. "The rest of us don't have your responsibilities. Now that Suzy is back, I've been let off the hook too."

Greco got to his feet and drew a large red question mark in the middle of the board. "We need to find who it is that belongs at the centre of all this."

Chapter 20

"You seen Geegee?" Les asked the lad as he walked into the Spinners.

"No. Been busy all day. Get me a pint," he asked feeling in his pocket for some money. "Coppers will have him again." He smirked. "They're trying to pin every crime in the city on him at the mo." He put a tenner on the counter and took hold of his beer. "Get me a whiskey to go with this and keep the change."

He saw the look. Les would be wondering why he was throwing his money around. Well, let him wonder. There'd be a whole lot more where that had come from soon enough. He looked around, the place was filling up. Mostly with Geegee's friends looking for a game. He laughed to himself; they were out of luck. But there were also those looking to buy drugs, and they might fare better.

He poured the whiskey into the beer and walked across to a bench by the front door. A group of young blokes had gathered there. They were waiting for Geegee. They needed their nightly fix. He could sort them but he wanted more than just a bit of casual dealing. The lad wanted the lot.

He planned to be the one the dealers came to, not just the users. He was going to be the man with the supply. As far as this town was concerned, and given time, the only man.

"He's not coming," the lad grinned at them. "So you're out of luck."

"He can't do this. We're regulars. He knows not to cross us."

"Geegee has . . . well, let's just say he's retired," he told them. "And he's passed the business over to me, lock stock and list of customers."

"So we buy off you — now that Geegee's gone?"

"Yeah." He leaned forward. "But not until I'm ready. Got it?"

They moved a few yards away from him. There was a lot of low mumbling with the occasional raised voice, and then one of them turned to the lad. "What do we call you?"

"Liam," he replied with a smile. It was the first time he'd ever used his birth name. "And tell your mates. You want dope, then from now on you deal with my people or you get nowt."

He checked the time. Nearly six, where was he? Five minutes later a voice rasped at him from the doorway.

"He won't come in. He wants you outside, in the car."

Liam didn't move. He didn't like to be told what to do and he didn't like to be kept waiting. Kashif Hussain needed to learn his new place in the scheme of things. But nonetheless he took hold of his drink and followed the young man outside. Kashif was sitting in the back of a gleaming white Mercedes. The young man opened the door and Liam slid in.

"You dealt with him?" Kashif began gruffly.

"Of course," he replied arrogantly. "Geegee won't be bothering anybody anymore. You — sorted your little problem with the police? You got out pretty quick, the cells not suit you?"

"How do you know about that?"

"Because I put you there," he replied coldly. "And without a swift attitude change I'll make sure you go right back."

"You can't do that. You don't have the power."

"Let me spell it out for you, Mr Hussain, so that we can avoid any unpleasantness in the future. The authorities think your little brother is involved in a terrorist plot. There is plenty of evidence, damning evidence too, but the authorities don't have it. Cross me and the police will get chapter and verse. Let me down, try anything clever and you will regret it. Tune in to the local news if you don't believe me," he offered with a snide smile. He paused, watching Kashif's face harden as he fought the urge to lose his temper.

Liam laughed, annoying Kashif even more. He was deliberately piling on the humiliation. "Young Tanweer has been keeping bad company. Currently they think you are at the bottom of it. Upset me and they will get all the proof they need to lock you both up for a very long time." He paused, giving Kashif time to mull this over. "Now, we'll try again. You have the customers and I have the supply. For now we merge, work things together."

"I've already got a supply. It has never failed me. So why should I get involved with you?"

"We've covered all this. Didn't you hear what I just said? Plus — you wanted rid of Gibbs. I've done that, so now you owe me. It's your turn to show some goodwill."

Kashif grunted.

"I hope you are not going back on our deal." Liam tutted. "I had a feeling — you being who you are — that would happen. So I took out some insurance. That insurance is your brother. After what he's been involved in today the police will watch your every move. You won't be able to sneeze without some cop writing it down. No, Mr Hussain, your days of bringing dope in through the docks are over. You are reliant on me now and I will run things my way." He stared at him for a moment, his eyes glittering with triumph. "So take it or leave it."

* * *

"Would you like to come round, eat with us?"

"I'm planning to work late," he explained to Suzy.

"I'll keep something for you. Matilda might be in bed but that'll give us the chance to talk. What do you say?"

"Okay, I'll come when I'm done here." He put the phone down.

Supper with his ex. A few weeks ago he'd never have believed it. That aside, unless they had some sort of breakthrough he wouldn't be very good company. His head was too full of possibilities. Grace had gone home, George too, leaving him, Quickenden and Craig. Quickenden had a bundle of statements and was ploughing through them again. Craig was on the computer trying to find out if there was a 'Liam Donnelly' living locally.

His phone rang. It was Julian Batho. "You working late too, Professor?"

"Indeed, and with a good outcome. I have finished processing some of the DNA results. As I suspected we found traces of DNA on Brenda Hirst's watch. The most numerous were those of Brenda Hirst herself, followed by Gibbs and Lily Dawson. However, there was another. The individual must have worn it and left a sweat trace. We don't have a match on the database but I can say with certainty that the DNA is from the offspring of both Gibbs and Rose. When I found a link to Gibbs I looked at Rose again and made that link too. It was your DC Harper who suggested it."

Grace had been right. The son, Liam Donnelly, was their killer but where was he? Had Rose known about him? Did he make contact with her? The questions were coming thick and fast but he had no answers. "Thank you, Professor. That gives us a name; all we have to do now is find him. If you find the same DNA on the laptop would you let me know at once?"

Greco went to the incident board and rubbed off the red question mark, replacing it with the name. He stood back and looked. Liam must have hated his parents with a passion to have done what he had. To seek vengeance in that way it must have festered in his head for years. But why Brenda? And what was the link with the bomb threats? If he could understand that, then he might stand a chance of finding him.

* * *

"I've made a vegetable lasagne. I even made the tomato sauce myself. Hope you're hungry."

Suzy seemed very jolly as she ushered him into her house. A far cry from the cold indifference he was used to.

"I might not be great company; bad day that's left me with more questions than I started with. But at least we've made some progress. We do have a prime suspect now."

"You do a good job, Stephen. You'll get your man, you always do," she assured him.

Not what he was used to hearing, either. "Have you been to work?"

"No, I'm still on leave but I will go back in a day or two."

"Is the job still to your liking?" he asked, taking the glass of wine she offered him.

"It's probably the only good thing to come out of the move. I love it," she confessed. "It's a good team and the department is on the up. We're offering a lot of new courses and there is no shortage of students."

"Sounds like hard work."

"It is. FE is so full on, but you know I like what I do. The job I had in Norwich was on the skids, the department was failing on all counts. Oldston has a large cohort of school leavers all looking for college courses."

"So you don't want to move back?"

"No." She smiled. "Don't get me wrong, I loved our home and the village we lived in. Oldston is so different and it takes some getting used to. Leesworth is nice though, and I like the hills. The villages around here are just as pretty as in Norfolk but in a different way."

"I'm glad you're happy," Greco said tucking in to the food she'd made.

"And you, Stephen? What do you intend to do?"

He shook his head. "I'm still not sure. This place is harsh, brutal. Don't misunderstand me, I've seen plenty in my time, but this place is so depressing."

"And what about our marriage?"

The question hung in the air between them.

"We're divorced, remember? Your idea; I simply rolled over and gave in."

"Perhaps you shouldn't have. Perhaps you should have fought."

"I doubt it would have got me anywhere. You had made your mind up and you didn't want to listen to my opinions." He shook his head. "Then you were gone. I didn't think I had any choice but to do as you'd decided."

"I do regret that now," she admitted, reaching for his hand. "I think I was probably ill, depressed. I wasn't thinking straight and leaving you is the biggest mistake I've ever made. I won't beg, Stephen but I want you back."

"I have a new job. It's tough but I am getting used to it and my new team. They're a bit rough around the edges but they've begun to show promise. You and me," he smiled at her, "we'll take things slow. I'm not going to change anything workwise just yet, so let's see what happens. You've met Grace's mum, Denise? She's a pleasant woman and Matilda likes her. Having her as backup will make things easier. We could go out. We could even try dating again."

He watched her laugh. Suzy looked happier than she had in months, and that was good. He was also beginning to feel better about things.

Chapter 21

Friday

"We need to find Liam Donnelly," Greco have Grace an approving look. "You were right. Your instincts were spot on." He tapped the name on the board. "Last night Craig searched the electoral roll for Oldston and the surrounding area and found nothing — no Liam Donnelly and as you said before, no Judith Calf. So if he is living here, then he's living under the radar."

"I don't understand why this Judith Calf claimed him all those years ago, if she wasn't his mother. But given that she did, she will have changed his name," Grace suggested.

That, unfortunately, was what Greco thought had happened.

"Gibbs and Rose were his parents. Recently he must have reconnected with Gibbs. He talked to him, went to his flat, and used his stuff. We don't know if Gibbs knew who he was but he must have trusted him." He raised an eyebrow at Quickenden.

"Geegee never trusted anyone, sir. It wasn't in his make-up. Everyone was fair game and there to be turned over. Like I said before, Geegee didn't make friends, he used people."

"Speedy, you saw him during the last weeks: who was he with? Did he say anything about finding his son? Was there anyone hanging around who was new, different from the others?"

"He called him Speedy again, did you hear?" Grace whispered to Craig.

"There was nothing unusual. It was the usual crew in the pub, the card school, the kids looking for dope and those who dip in and out for a drink. There never is anyone new. The Spinners isn't that type of pub. You wouldn't take your latest bird there, for example." Quickenden paused for a second. "But there was the lad, I'd completely forgotten about him. Remember, the one who told me about the watch Geegee was trying to flog. He was new, never seen him before."

Greco shook his head. "How many times have I asked the question, Sergeant? Why didn't you recall this earlier?"

"I did mention the lad," he excused.

"But you didn't say he was someone new, did you?"

"I don't think he is. I've seen him around, just not in the pub."

"So Liam Donnelly isn't new to the area, just new to the Spinners. He's someone who is always there, someone everyone knows and doesn't notice, like background noise."

There was murmuring as this idea took root.

"So Liam knew Gibbs but Gibbs had no idea who he was?" Grace postulated.

"It looks like that. If a son turned up out of the blue then I'm sure Geegee would have boasted about it," Quickenden told them.

"There is something else, something I've not told you yet," Greco interrupted. "The laptop taken from Gibbs's flat was used to send the emails warning about both the bomb scare in the shopping centre and the device on the coach."

Now there was silence. He had all their attention now. He'd had to tell them; Greco needed their input. They'd find out sooner or later and Liam Donnelly had to be caught before he killed someone else. "Why would Gibbs get involved with something like that? What would he hope to gain?"

"Well, he wouldn't." Quickenden looked puzzled. "He doesn't have the know-how for a start. And he wasn't interested in anything like that. All that terrorist stuff is way over his head. All Geegee wanted was to make money as easily as possible, and in his world that meant dealing."

"So are we to assume it was Liam who got him involved? But if Gibbs didn't know who Liam was why would he go along with the plot? He must have thought it worth his while or he'd have left it alone."

Greco heard Quickenden's fingers click as the penny dropped.

"Drugs, sir, that's what this is about. If you think about it, then it all fits. Incriminate the Hussains, drop them right in it and the coast is clear. Geegee would move in and take over hassle free. I'll lay odds that having Tanweer Hussain involved was deliberate. Some clever bastard has really thought this one through and believe me that wasn't Geegee. The stupid thug was set up with the promise of inheriting the lot."

"The Hussains run the tobacco scam and the drugs?" Greco queried.

"That family are at the top of the chain. Geegee has always done okay but all he really gets is the crumbs from their table. Get rid of them and everything falls apart. When that happens the way is open for someone to move in and take control. Liam Donnelly aided by Geegee is my bet."

"Kashif Hussain's supply?"

"With his family in the frame for planting the device, they won't be able to operate. They'll be watched. Someone like Geegee could've cleaned up."

"But he's no longer with us. So — who else? The Hussains are out of the picture and so is Grady Gibbs. That leaves the path clear for a takeover."

"Sir, someone has planned this carefully. If it is Liam Donnelly, then he's got rid of his parents and he wants the drugs operation in this town for himself — all of it. That means getting rid of the Hussains as well. It looks to me as if he's done that and very effectively too."

"If the Hussains can't operate, then where would the supply come from to enable a takeover?" Craig asked, confused.

"At this time we've no idea but the bastard will have that worked out, bound to have," Quickenden answered.

"We'll bring Kashif Hussain in again. From what I've read in the reports about him, his one weakness is his family. He'll not be happy that Tanweer is part of this."

"Shall I go, sir?" volunteered Quickenden. "Me and Craig will go and get him."

"Yes, but don't tell him anything. He'll know Tanweer is involved but don't mention Gibbs or anyone else." He looked at Grace, and Georgina who'd just joined them. "Sixteen years ago, a woman in this town heard the radio broadcast about the missing child and claimed him. It seems reasonable to assume that she used a false name. Grace, see if the hospital still has records of women seeking fertility treatment. It's a long shot, but you never know. I'll get the legal stuff put in place."

"Sir," George interrupted. "Alex Reader has turned up."

That was something at least. "Where is he?"

"In the soft interview room waiting for you, sir."

* * *

Alex Reader sat staring at his feet. He didn't look well. From the state of his clothing Greco got the impression that he'd been sleeping rough or in that car of his.

"I wasn't arrested," he began, on seeing Greco enter the room. "I came in voluntarily."

"What I don't understand, Mr Reader, is why you ran in the first place."

"Because of the questions, the stuff you'd try to pin on me, if you knew the truth," was his sullen reply.

"That's not how we work, Mr Reader." Greco watched the man shuffle nervously as he considered this. "So what is it you haven't told me?"

"You know about Brenda and me."

"You had no reason to run because of that."

"There is more. I haven't told you everything. The row we had that Saturday was worse than I made out. She screamed at me and I lost it."

"Did you strike her?"

"No, nothing like that, but it was because of me that she got out of the car. I was shouting at her. She wouldn't leave me alone. She wanted me to leave my wife and live somewhere with her. I said no, I didn't want her. The baby was a mistake; I thought I'd made myself clear and that she understood." He shook his head. "But she didn't, she wouldn't stop going on about how happy we could be. I got really riled." He fell silent.

"Are you sure you didn't harm her?"

"No, but I did follow her. She'd left her shopping in the boot so I ran after her with the two bags. Brenda was crying, she didn't know where she was going. She screamed at me, told me to get lost. She wandered onto the canal bank; then another woman heard the shouting and approached us."

"What woman? Did you know her?"

He hung his head. "Yes, because she'd been in my showroom looking at cars. She wanted me to look out for a particular model for her."

"So who was she?"

"Rose Donnelly."

That meant that Alex Reader had been on the canal bank that afternoon with both Brenda and Rose. Brenda wasn't seen alive after that — but what about Rose?

"What happened next?"

"Rose Donnelly went to help Brenda. She gave me a right mouthful and told me to get lost. I tried to explain, but she was in no mood to listen."

"What was she doing there, did she say?"

"No, but there was someone else, a young bloke in overalls. He was coming over the bridge from the other side of the canal. He shouted to Brenda and she waved back. I got the impression that she knew him."

"Do you know who he was?"

Reader shook his head. "No, but he had fair hair, and like I said, he was wearing overalls. I thought perhaps he'd come from one of the workshops along there, you know, the ones near mine."

"What did you do then?"

"I put the shopping at her feet and left them to it."

"And you ran because you thought this information would somehow incriminate you?"

"Yes. You asked me about Rose Donnelly. You only had to realise that her and Brenda had been on the canal bank with me that day and that'd be it."

Greco shook his head.

* * *

"Did he explain himself?" Grace asked, as Greco entered the office.

"A little. Rose was on the canal bank at the same time as Brenda and they may have been joined by a young man in overalls," he said, as he wrote all this on the incident board.

"Are we keeping him, is he a suspect?"

204

"No, the killings have nothing to do with him." He tapped the name on the board. "This is who we need to speak to."

"Social services are couriering over the records about him, sir," she told him.

Knowing more about Liam Donnelly was one thing, but that was obviously not the name he was living under or they would have found him. What they really needed to know was who he was now.

"Where's Sergeant Quickenden gone?" He asked seeing the empty desk.

"Speedy said he wanted to follow up on something, sir. He left about half an hour ago."

Chapter 22

Speedy was counting on Darren Hopper not being aware of the full extent of what he'd got mixed up in. The lad wasn't that bright and he got by doing the dirty work of others, but this time he'd been dropped right in it. He had nowhere to go, so the chances were that he'd be holed up at home until things quietened.

He parked outside the block and waited. Stace, Daz's girlfriend, appeared with the kid in a pushchair and walked off in the direction of the shops. This was his chance.

He bounded up the stairs and rapped on the door. He could hear noise coming from inside the flat. Someone had the radio on and they were singing.

"What's up, forget something?" came a male voice, opening the front door.

Daz Hopper had a grin on his face but that rapidly melted away when he saw Speedy.

"You've been a naughty boy," the sergeant said, shaking his head. "Do you listen to anything else except that crap?" He nodded at the radio. "You heard the news lately?"

Daz shook his head as he pulled a T-shirt over his bare chest.

"Well, you should, because mostly it's been all about you, you and that stupid mate of yours, Tanweer."

"We ain't done nowt," he snapped back. "You can't just come here and pin stuff on me."

"You took a trip on one of Webb's coaches. You scarpered leaving your bags in the hold." He moved closer and stared into Daz's face. "There was a bomb in one of those bags. Did you know that, Darren?"

The young man flinched and jumped back in surprise. "No way, man! That had absolutely nothing to do with us. We were just doing . . ." Then he shut up.

"Doing what, Darren? What you were told? And who was it issuing the orders?"

"I can't tell you, he'll kill me."

"No, he won't because he's dead. Murdered." That news really shook Daz. He staggered back and flopped onto a chair. He obviously had no idea.

"The police and God knows who have been looking for you. Where have you been?"

"Keeping out of the way," he replied. "Stace's mother's mostly."

"I want you to come down to the station with me and give a statement."

"And if I don't?"

"Then I'll arrest you." Quickenden phoned for a police car to come and pick him up. "Where's your mate?"

"Don't know, I haven't seen or heard from him since we got back. I reckon Kashif is hiding him somewhere."

Speedy needed to tell Greco. That particular nut might be a bit more difficult to crack.

* * *

"Good work, Sergeant, but you don't go off on your own without telling us or better still, taking someone with you. Got that?"

"Sorry, sir, I was acting on a hunch — and it paid off." He smiled proudly at the others. "Darren Hopper isn't the brightest; he was easily found and picked up."

"He can rest up in the cells for a while and then we'll speak to him. For the time being Mr Kashif Hussain is waiting to be interviewed."

"Want me in on that one, sir?"

"Okay, but don't say anything out of turn. He's got his lawyer with him. A designer-suited so and so from Manchester."

Kashif Hussain was sitting calmly beside his solicitor. He looked up as the two detectives entered the room and shook his head.

"You are wasting your time and mine. I have nothing else to say. You have got this wrong. What happened on that coach has nothing to do with me or my family."

"I'm afraid that's where you're wrong, Mr Hussain. There are dozens of witnesses to testify that your younger brother was on that coach. Once we catch him, I'm sure it'll be his fingerprints we find all over one of those cases."

Kashif fixed Greco with a stare. "Tanweer was not involved. He was fitted up to make it look that way. He was with me at the time, doing work for our uncle."

"Whether you choose to believe me or not, Tanweer was on that coach and he was involved. He will be arrested and a jury will convict him. Anyone who is found to be harbouring him will suffer the same fault. So I'll ask you again, do you know where he is?"

Kashif Hussain looked at Greco. "No, and even if I did, I wouldn't tell you. You have nothing. You have a bag with fingerprints on it but you have no proof that they are Tanweer's." He looked at his lawyer. "I want to leave."

"Why would someone want to incriminate Tanweer in something like this?"

"I have no idea."

"Well, we've given it some thought and we think someone out there wants to ensure that your family can no longer operate . . . certain aspects of your business."

"I have no idea what you mean."

"I think you do. I think you know very well that this will put an end to the drug smuggling. Your family is now marked and you'll be watched. Whatever scam you were running to get drugs into the country is out the window."

Kashif said something to his lawyer in Urdu.

"The drug business is what this is all about. That and a little personal matter someone wanted settled. I think you and your family have been used, Mr Hussain. In the popular vernacular, you've been shafted."

"No one does that to me," he retorted with venom. "No one uses my family. People in this town know better."

"Well, that's what's happened, isn't it?" He gave the man a moment or two to think about it. "Tanweer was set up and now the shadow of suspicion has fallen on you and your entire business operation." Greco leaned back and folded his arms. "That leaves the coast clear for a new face to step in."

"Rubbish! This is pure guesswork. You have nothing, admit it!"

Greco shrugged — the man was right. "Okay, Mr Hussain, you can go."

"You have him rattled, sir," Quickenden said, once Kashif and his lawyer had left the room.

"That was the whole idea, Sergeant. Now I want him watched. One of the team and a uniformed officer at all times. He is hiding his brother. I'd lay odds on it and I'm not a betting man."

They went back to the main office, Craig was on the phone. "Sir, Professor Batho has been on. He says he'll have the sample from Webb's analysed today."

"Good work, Craig."

"Speedy, work out a rota for keeping tabs on Kashif and get on with it straight away." Greco sat at his desk. He had one thing on his mind. Who was Liam Donnelly? There was no guarantee that either Darren Hopper or Tanweer would know any more than he did. They needed a break. He'd go and speak to Darren Hopper.

* * *

"Look, I'm not being fitted up for any terrorist thing," he said to Greco as he was brought into the interview room. "It was just a drop for Geegee. I thought drugs, guns, something like that. We weren't told nothing."

"Did you usually do Gibbs's dirty work?"

"He could go crazy if you didn't do as he said. Anyway he was paying us a ton each."

"Did Gibbs tell you anything about what was going on, what he was into?"

"No, but then he wouldn't. I was just another of his errand boys."

"How did you get the luggage?"

"He told me to go round to his flat. He gave me the luggage and the disguises."

"Was he alone there? Did he give any hint at any time that anyone else was involved?"

"Never saw no one, and that's the truth."

"Are you sure? No strangers, no face you didn't recognise?"

He watched Darren think.

"He was into some dodgy stuff on that computer of his. He said he used the dark web to Skype his mates, only it wasn't Skype. I saw one of them, a blonde lad with odd-coloured eyes. Weird-looking, he was."

"Did he say who he was?"

"Geegee wouldn't say, just that if the lad thought I could recognise him again, he'd kill me."

"Did you get the impression that this lad was involved? Did Gibbs say anything?"

He watched Darren shrug. "He said nowt but I suppose he must have been. I never really gave it much thought. I just wanted the dosh to pay the rent."

"Have you ever seen this person before?"

"No, I don't think so."

Greco could see the doubt on Darren's face. He was holding back.

"But you're not sure?"

"I think he might have been in the Spinners but I can't be sure."

"What did you mean by *odd-coloured* eyes?"

"They were different colours; one was blue and the other brown."

That would certainly help in identifying someone.

"Okay, Darren, we're going to keep you here for a while longer. I have colleagues from another department who will no doubt want a word."

* * *

Back in the office, Greco wrote the words 'odd eyes' on the board. They might belong to Liam or they might not. It could have been anyone's face on that laptop.

Chapter 23

"Anything on Tanweer Hussain yet?" Greco asked Grace.

"No, sir. That family is sitting tight. All their shops are closed except for Nazir's and no one is dealing. With them out of action and Gibbs dead, the town will be wild later."

"I'll tell the super, we may need extra bodies on the street. Where is Quickenden?"

"He's gone down to the canteen for something to eat." Grace smiled. "He's learned his lesson. He won't be doing any more runners, sir."

Craig was statement-shuffling again and George was sitting in front of her computer.

Julian Batho called on the office phone.

"Inspector, I have some information for you. The oil from Webb's workshop matches that from under Brenda Hirst's fingernails. They use thick grease for lubrication; so it's different from the others."

So their killer was someone from Webb's. He looked at the board — Webb's coaches were already up there. They were involved, but how? He needed to think. The Judith Calf thing was bothering him. The woman hadn't appeared out of nowhere. Back then she'd heard the news on the local radio and for some reason decided to claim the child as her own. Greco sat at his desk. He had an idea. He accessed a site he'd used many times in his family history research. Within minutes he'd determined that a woman with that name hadn't given birth to a child during the time frame they were looking at. Next he accessed marriage data. He checked back several years and there it was — bingo!

"Twenty-five years ago, a Judith Calf got married in Oldston," he announced to the team. "It was a long shot but I wondered if the woman who claimed Liam might have used her maiden name."

He could see from the look on Grace's face that she was impressed. George and Craig both stopped what they were doing and stared at him.

"Who did she marry?" Craig asked.

"Percival Webb," he told them all. "And there is no record of the Webb's ever having a child of their own. So Liam Donnelly must have become Nathan Webb." Greco looked around at the heads all nodding. "What do we know about him?"

"Not a lot. He doesn't have any sort of police record. He's a hard-working young man with moneyed parents and a promising future," Grace told them. "So why get mixed up in that lot?" She nodded at the board.

"Because he harboured resentment and hate, probably all his life," Greco surmised. "We need to pick him up."

"What's going on?" Quickenden asked, just then coming into the office.

Greco nodded at the board. "We know who he is."

Greco watched Quickenden move closer to read the new notes. "Odd-coloured eyes . . . I've seen a pair of strange eyes recently . . ." He thought for a moment. "In the Spinners the other day. That new kid I told you about, he was waiting for Geegee. It must be him — he must be this Liam."

"You and I will take a ride over to Webb's workshop, see if he's there. Grace and Craig, you two go and have a word with Mrs Webb, see what she has to say."

"How did you find him, sir? I was only gone half an hour or so."

"It was down to a hunch."

"I didn't think you liked hunches, sir."

"An educated hunch, Sergeant, the one about women using their maiden names in certain situations."

* * *

The Webb family lived in a huge, rambling stone house on the outskirts of Oldston. It was surrounded by a high fence and the gate was locked. Grace pressed the button and waited.

"DCs Harper and Merrick from Oldston CID," she told the male voice who answered.

Moments later the gate sprung open and they were able to drive in. "Some pile they've got," Craig noted.

"Business must be good. It's a shame that we have to do this. I wonder if Liam's given them much aggro over the years. He's such a troubled young man I can't see life with him being sweet, can you?"

"Is it about Brenda?" Percival Webb greeted them at the door. "It really shook everyone up, losing her like that."

"Is your wife in, Mr Webb?" Grace asked with a smile.

"Judith? Well, yes, come on in," he offered.

Judith Webb met them in the hall. She was about fifty years old. Her hair was greying, she was thin and she looked twitchy.

"This is about Nathan," Grace began, "or perhaps I should call him Liam."

Grace watched her reaction closely. Judith Webb's expression did not change. She stared silently at both detectives for several seconds and then she looked at her husband.

"They know," she almost whispered.

"We know that he isn't your biological son, and we know who he really is. We need to find him. Liam has done things, terrible things, so we need to stop him before he does anything else."

Grace saw the tears, the woman was upset. "I didn't think I was doing anything wrong."

"He wasn't your child, Mrs Webb."

"No, but he wasn't wanted by his real parents. We couldn't have children of our own, and we were desperate," sobbed Judith. "He was unwanted, ill-treated, but such a lovely little boy. When I heard the local news on the radio that day I had to do something, so I decided to take him." She shrugged. "It was easy. I went to the police station and spoke to the officer on the desk. He brought Liam through to sit with me. We sat on a bench; I'd taken some toys and a bag of sweets. We chatted as we waited, I read him a story. They were very busy that day, there had been a robbery I think and everyone was called away. Me and Liam sat there in that draughty room for ages, but no one came. Eventually he fell asleep. I'd given the officer on the desk a false name. I know I was wrong but I was desperate for a child. We'd tried everything and got nowhere," she explained as if it justified her actions. "Finally, I picked him up and took him out. No one came after us, we simply walked away. We raised him as our own. No one ever came looking and Liam seemed happy. We sent him to school and provided everything he wanted. One day he'll inherit the business."

"Where is he, Mr Webb?" Craig asked. "He'll be at the workshop." He went to stand beside his wife.

Craig took his phone and rang Greco.

Grace thought the whole incident sounded extraordinary. Why wasn't the boy's welfare followed up on? There must be more to it, but this was not the time to find out more.

* * *

It was late afternoon and getting dark. The workshop was bathed in fluorescent light as they approached. "Park behind that truck." Greco pointed. "We don't want him to see us coming."

"Backup is on the way. They are blocking off the surrounding roads too. If he does do a runner then he's got nowhere to go."

Liam Donnelly had a hosepipe in his hand and was washing down a coach. He didn't hear them approach and turned as one of the mechanics called out.

"What do you want?" His tone was sour. "We're about to close up, can't it wait until Monday?"

"This is not a business visit, Nathan, we're the police." Greco showed the young man his badge. "We want you to come with us, answer a few questions."

"You're wasting your time because I know nowt."

"We've spoken to Mrs Webb, we know the truth about who you are," Greco told him. "Look at me, Liam."

* * *

Liam Donnelly turned slowly, dropped the hose and his odd-coloured eyes looked straight into Greco's. This was the moment he'd been half expecting. He was clever; he could always get one over on the likes of the Hussains and Geegee, but the police were bound to be a close match for him. "I don't care," he smiled. "I got them and they suffered plenty for what they did to me."

"Rose and Gibbs?"

"Sounds like a firm of solicitors." His laugh was almost demented. "But they were far from that. They were my parents, can you believe that?" There was more manic laughter. "But joking apart, they were evil, the pair of them. I wanted to get back at them for screwing up my life." He took a rag and started to clean the oil from his hands. "I planned and schemed with the worst of them. I did it well too. Shame about the drugs, though. I was set to be the new *Mr Big* around here," he told them proudly. "I've stuffed the Hussains, big style." He looked at Greco. "But you know that, don't you, copper? A clever bloke like you — bet you've worked it all out."

"Eventually," Greco allowed. "The bomb scares?"

"Me, all me. My way of getting rid of Kashif and his cronies."

"No real terrorists, then?"

"Not this time. Good plan though, don't you think? Bomb in the luggage put in the hold of a coach. That system of doing things needs tightening up. A traveller doesn't come back after a stop and the coach just continues — luggage left where it is. Big with possibilities that one."

"Brenda Hirst — why kill her?"

"She stumbled onto the canal bank just as I was meeting Rose. I'd already given Rose something to make her — well, let's just say, more amenable. Brenda got in the way. So I clobbered her."

"You took her eyes, like with the others."

"I like eyes," he smiled. "They're my hobby. I collect them, you know."

"You need to come with us now, Liam."

* * *

"He's as mad as a hatter," Quickenden decided as he came back from the cells. "He thinks he's done well. He doesn't see it at all."

"I'm just glad it's all over," Grace added, leaning back on her chair and closing her eyes. "What about you, sir?"

"Absolutely." He was looking at the incident board. "You all did very well in the end."

Greco was particularly impressed with Grace. She'd contributed a lot to the case. Far from being one of the no-hopers, she had a future. Quickenden he wasn't so sure about. The jury was still out on that one. Craig Merrick was a plodder and so was George. He'd see if the next case could ignite a spark before he made any decisions about their futures with the team.

"Coming for a drink with us, sir? It is Friday night." Craig asked.

Greco was about to refuse. After all, he always did. But they were all looking at him expectantly. This case had changed something within the dynamic of the team. *Team* — yes; perhaps now they might be.

"Okay, but just one. I'll give Suzy a ring first; tell her I'll be late."

The End

Thank you for reading this book. If you enjoyed it please leave feedback on Amazon, and if there is anything we missed or you have a question about then please get in touch. The author and publishing team appreciate your feedback and time reading this book.

Our email is jasper@joffebooks.com

www.joffebooks.com

ALSO BY HELEN DURRANT

CALLADINE & BAYLISS MYSTERIES
DEAD WRONG
DEAD SILENT
DEAD LIST
DEAD LOST

DI GRECO
DARK MURDER

17589952R00134

Printed in Great Britain
by Amazon